This book  the
Mid York **W9-AWL-566**

**When you are finished reading,
please return the book so
that others may enjoy it.**

The Mid York Library System is pleased
to partner with **CABVI** in assisting
those with special vision needs.

If you found the size of print in this book
helpful, there may be other ways
CABVI can help. Please call today toll
free at **1-877-719-9996**
or **(315) 797-2233**.

cabvi
Central Association for the Blind and Visually Impaired

Mid York
LIBRARY SYSTEM

MID-YORK Library System
1600 Lincoln Avenue Utica, New York 13502

Walk a Tightrope

Walk a Tightrope

JULIE ELLIS

G.K. Hall & Co. • Chivers Press
Waterville, Maine USA Bath, England

This Large Print edition is published by G.K. Hall & Co., USA and by Chivers Press, England.

Published in 2002 in the U.S. by arrangement with Julie Ellis.

Published in 2002 in the U.K. by arrangement with the author.

U.S. Hardcover   0-7838-9737-5 (Romance Series)
U.K. Hardcover   0-7540-4802-0 (Chivers Large Print)

Copyright © 1975 by Julie Ellis

All rights reserved.

The text of this Large Print edition is unabridged.
Other aspects of the book may vary from the original edition.

Set in 16 pt. Plantin.

Printed in the United States on permanent paper.

British Library Cataloguing in Publication Data available

ISBN 0-7838-9737-5

For Robin, Neil, and Russy

Chapter One

Jill Conrad walked to the closet in the bedroom of the fourth-floor brownstone apartment she shared with her roommate, Sheila. She pulled out a coat, bent to draw out a pair of boots, crossed to the window to gaze out into the night.

Why did she feel so depressed, almost fearful? She ought to be bursting with exhilaration. Tonight she was opening in her first off-Broadway play.

Snow-draped Stuyvesant Park was deserted as far as Jill could see, except for a pair of cold-immune drunks who shared a bottle on a bench. The early evening dog-walkers, attuned to the dangers of city parks, remained on the outside of the wrought iron fence surrounding the park, which tonight had a postcard beauty with its yet untrampled snow bathed in the spill of light from the splendor of St. George's Church.

Jill glanced at the clock atop St. George's. Almost an hour before she was due at the playhouse. But she'd go stir-crazy if she stayed here much longer. Go on to the playhouse. It would be open. The stage crew would still be working, even though the opening was tonight.

After all the agonizing months of making

rounds, of endless evenings of classes and studio performances, of reading unsuccessfully for parts, she would, at last, set foot on a stage and be paid for it. A shoestring, off-Broadway production, but it made her a professional.

Only in unguarded moments did she admit to herself that the New York theater rat race unnerved, terrified her. She'd come to New York because at college it had been hammered into her mind that here was the center of the action.

How she loathed walking into casting offices, clutching her manila envelope stuffed with photos and padded resumes. Wearing the bright, false smile that was part of the act. Seeing the same bright, false smiles all around her. Some of these kids were brashly confident, sure they were going to make it to the top. Some had a special drive — but most of them were like her. In six months or a year most of them walked out on the rat race, and some went back home.

But Jill's father had begun a whole new life — he was on a special assignment in Peru. And the house in which she had grown up had been sold to a corporate executive transferred from Phoenix.

"Sheila —" Jill called to her roommate.

Jill hovered in the doorway to the small, square living room. Slim, fair-haired, brown-eyed. Skin milk white, easy to color becomingly. Features fine. The dark eyes appealingly wistful, owing this charm to mild myopia.

8

"You're not going to the theater already?" Sheila looked up in astonishment from the manuscript she had brought home from the office to read. She was a junior editor for Dobson Books.

"I know it's early, but I want to get made up, and just sit around and go over lines in my mind."

"You were great at the dress rehearsal last night," Sheila said enthusiastically. Last night friends of the cast had been guests.

"I hope the reviewers think so." Jill's smile was wry. The only place she had proved herself great so far, except for college performances, was as a typist for the temporary agency that sent her out religiously three days a week and tried to coax her into working five. Those two days belonged to round-making, possible auditions. "I hope the reviewers show up." They would. Elaine Mitchell, their producer, had the requisite union publicist included in their stringent budget. That guaranteed a certain amount of stock publicity. "Of course, my part's awfully small."

"It's showy," Sheila encouraged. "You came over real. I believed you."

Jill sat down, pulled on her boots, trying to cope with opening-night nerves. She had two scenes. One of them was terrific. Two of the kids in the cast had agents coming down. With an agent interested in you, there was a chance of making it into a Broadway show. Into a movie being shot in New York. Into TV.

9

Why couldn't she be aggressive like some of the others? Why did she die a little each time she walked into an office? But with an agent it was so much easier. Let something happen from this production.

"Break a leg." Sheila smiled reassuringly. "I know you'll be great."

"I won't be home till late." Jill tried to sound casual. "We'll probably go somewhere afterward and tear the performance apart." And pretend they weren't sitting around for the early editions of the *Times* and the *News*, waiting hopefully for good reviews.

The play wasn't sure-fire, Jill acknowledged to herself, walking down the narrow, dimly lit three flights to the front door. The cast of seven kept telling themselves it was, because you had to believe in the script if you were to give your best. But they had all been conscious of holes during rehearsal. Rewrites had helped a little, but four weeks' rehearsal was too brief to polish a script.

Scott said Hal would make it big as a playwright one day. But not with this script. Scott was twenty-three and feeling his way. He'd met Elaine Mitchell, sixtyish and rich, when he was teaching ballroom dancing during a lean period — and sold her on turning producer.

Scott was realistic. The play was a showcase. Rehearsal money was peanuts, and the salary, guaranteed by the Equity bond, unimpressive. But it was a stepping stone. Scott had been in half a dozen off-Broadway productions. He'd picked up a TV commercial as a result of one, and the residuals from it kept him living for a year.

The night was cold, damp. Jill buttoned her coat up to her chin, walked with shoulders hunched against the March cold to Second Avenue. She moved cautiously because not every segment of sidewalk had been cleaned of snow, and treacherous pockets of ice could trap the unwary.

Tonight she would take the bus, even though the playhouse was only a few blocks south. Second Avenue after dark was a frightening area for her, with the drunks and addicts increasingly in evidence. Dad had been nervous about her coming to New York, after all he'd read about the dangers of living in the city, yet she knew he was relieved that she was building a place for herself. He'd delayed his marriage to Anne for over a year because he was concerned for her.

At the corner of Fifteenth Street, under the comforting brightness of the street lights, Jill paused, spying a cab just beyond, at the traffic light. All right, be a spendthrift tonight. She lifted a gloved hand to hail the cab just as the light changed from red to green.

The cab moved down Second Avenue, making all the lights, depositing her at the corner she'd indicated. She walked from Second Avenue along the dark street, between low rows of tenements. The entrance to the theater was brilliantly lighted already to lure ticket-buyers. Not for tonight's performance, though. The ninety-nine seats were all carefully allotted. Most of them "paper," to accommodate reviewers, agents, friends of the producer.

Jill walked past the box office, past the display of cast photos, into the theater. Onstage, Elaine Mitchell was supervising the hanging of a group of Manet prints, whose position at last night's dress rehearsal had displeased her. This was an expensive toy. Let Elaine achieve what pleasure she could from the production.

Jill walked noiselessly to the door beside the tiny stage, which led to the dressing rooms. In reality, one long, narrow area with a curtain dividing actors from actresses. A curtain that nobody had bothered to close in the excitement of last night's dress rehearsal. At such moments, Jill thought with humor, a cast was unisex.

"Hi." Scott, matinee idol handsome in his mid-twenties, glanced up from a place at the long makeup table that he'd staked out as his own. She'd forgot Scott would be here early. He wanted plenty of time to work with his beard. "I didn't expect you for forty minutes."

"I couldn't sit around the apartment any longer." Scott was so sweet. She'd seen a lot of him these four weeks of rehearsal. Not just at the playhouse. Afterward. Sitting around the cafeteria over coffee, or up in somebody's apartment over more coffee. They were all too involved in the production to be concerned about their personal lives; yet every time Scott looked at her, he told her she was special.

It would be so easy to fall in love with Scott. Because she was lonely. Because she was uneasy in this huge, strange city, even after all these months. Was she already in love with Scott? No, don't think about that. Not now. Not until after the opening.

She reached for her first-act dress, left the dressing room to change in the washroom. She couldn't be as casual as the others yet about the communal dressing room. Changing, she ran over her lines in her mind. Feeling a painful touch of panic as curtain time neared. Let her not blow her lines, go blank onstage!

By the time she returned to the dressing room Scott had finished with his beard, was complacently admiring the results. She slid onto the long bench in front of the mirror, reached into her make-up kit for the Albolene. Not a college audience out there tonight. New Yorkers. Accustomed to the best in theater.

The cast took four group curtain calls. Courtesy of their friends, Scott said grimly as they walked into the dressing room.

"You don't think they liked it?" Jill asked shakily. What rotten luck, to have her main scene cut down to four lines because Bill jumped.

"It's got some good spots," Scott conceded, "but not enough of them. We'll run a week, anyway." It had startled her to see the closing

13

notice posted before the curtain went up; but Scott explained this was routine, to cover the producer in case she wanted to close at the end of the week. "You can run uptown and try to browbeat an agent into coming down to see you if you get a good review." He reached for her hand. "Relax. You've come through your opening performance. You're a pro."

The dressing room chatter was high-pitched, strained, ranging from abject pessimism to unbridled enthusiasm for the performance. Elaine Mitchell, in a floor-length dress thirty years too young, darted with quick, small steps into the dressing room.

"Cast, we've all been invited out for supper by a member of the audience," she announced effusively. Between acts Elaine had served coffee from an urn in the lobby, which provided for brief socializing. "He thought you all worked terribly hard." Scott mumbled a dry assessment of this comment. Jill glanced anxiously at Elaine. She hadn't heard. "We'll meet out front."

With the prospect of supper at Ratner's ahead of them, the cast speedily assembled in the minute lobby. Elaine Mitchell, clinging to her restless playwright, was talking with a slender sixtyish man with near-white hair. There was a gentle, diffident air about him as he listened with dark, intelligent eyes to what Elaine was telling him about Hal's background. A listener rather than a talker, Jill guessed.

14

"Hal could be making a lot of money in paperbacks, but he's a theater man. He must be true to himself." She smiled speculatively at her listener. "Are you in the arts, Mr. Danzig?"

"No." His faint smile widened to welcome the cluster of actors and actresses that gathered about him. "I manufacture farm tools." A note of apology in his voice, Jill thought, because he earned his living so far from the arts.

Jill was drawn to Frank Danzig almost at once. There was a love of theater, a love of people, she felt, in him. So many of those she encountered in round-making intimidated her with their brashness, their "look at me, I'm beautiful" attitude. She loved being part of a play, taking lines and making them come to life. Being somebody else for those hours of rehearsal and performance. She cherished the rapport with an audience that came sometimes. It would come more often as she learned her craft.

They were moving en masse onto the sidewalk. Tramping over the city-ugly snow toward Second Avenue, to head north to Ratner's. Danzig listening with interest to the theater talk that spurted around him, but often his eyes moved to Jill.

"You were good," he said quietly to Jill as he fell into step beside Scott and her as they broke up into groups. "You both were." But Jill felt he was including Scott perfunctorily. "I believed you." Sheila, too, had said that.

"What about the play?" Scott asked. "You see

a lot of theater," he surmised. "How does it stand up?"

"I come to New York three times a year, for ten-day visits," Frank told them with quiet satisfaction. "To see the plays, go through the museums, roam about the bookstores. This play has some good moments," he acknowledged cautiously. "I'm not a critic, but I doubt that it will go uptown."

He was being kind. He obviously doubted that it would go beyond a week. It was going to start all over again. Three days typing, two days making rounds. The constant tension, and driving herself into offices. But Scott said they'd make rounds together. With Scott it would be easier.

They all went into the restaurant. A Second Avenue landmark, Elaine had said. Once Jill had been here with Scott at their lunch break. Usually, they had hamburgers from paper bags, drank their coffee from sagging containers. This once they'd splurged, dined among the TV people who'd wandered down from the Central Plaza rehearsal studios.

A pair of waiters pushed tables together to accommodate their party. Elaine coyly prodded Frank into a chair at the head of the table, dropped into a chair beside him, with Hal at her other side. At Danzig's gentle, unobtrusive maneuvering Jill and Scott sat at his other side.

"Don't you get terribly lonely up there in Maine?" Elaine leaned forward, gazing at him

16

seductively through her false eyelashes. "A man with your artistic inclinations?"

"I work at my plant," Danzig said tightly. "I have no time to be lonely." But Elaine had struck a raw nerve, Jill sensed.

"Three times a year," he reminded her, "I come down to New York. In ten days I see twelve to fifteen plays. How many New Yorkers see that many in a year? And lately, I have regular guests from the city." He took a deep breath, his eyes reflective. "Almost two years ago I had a heart attack. It scared me. I decided to do some of the things that give me real pleasure." Jill listened attentively. "I have a large house high on a cliff overlooking the Atlantic. Long before I bought it, it was named Cliff House."

"How romantic," Elaine said effusively. "Is it darkly Victorian and slightly frightening?"

"Victorian, yes. Hardly romantic or frightening," he demurred with a faint smile. "I've opened it up as a kind of retreat for creative people who need a breathing spell. I feel that people get lost sometimes in the everyday business of living; and in my house by the sea they can find themselves again, if they give themselves a chance. That's why I ask that whoever comes up remain for at least four weeks. To give my house a fair chance." His eyes were dark with intensity as they swept the faces around him. He knows I'm tense, Jill thought. That I'm not comfortable in this scene.

"If any of you feel a need to escape the city, for

17

a few weeks or a few months, you're welcome to come up as my guest. I can accommodate up to five at a time. Right now I have four guests." He reached into his jacket for a card, his eyes lingering on Jill. A house by the sea, she thought. Beautiful silences. "Here's my address and phone number up in Maine. Just call me. And if there's a vacant room, I'll be delighted to have you. Call me after seven," he cautioned, "when I'll be home from the plant."

Jill slid Frank Danzig's card into her wallet. He made his money in prosaic tool manufacturing, but he opened his house to people in the arts who were foundering. To bring the creative world, in some small fashion, into his life.

Jill listened with a strange inner excitement as Frank talked about Cliff House. About the austere beauty of Maine winters. About his current guests, all of whom he had met casually on one or another of his jaunts into Manhattan.

He's lonely, she thought with compassion. He's desperately lonely.

They sat over more cups of coffee in discussion clusters of twos and threes while the tables about them were gradually deserted. The tension that kept them stiff in their chairs was communal.

Jill was intrigued to discover that Frank's favorite playwrights, despite their disparity, were her own. Eugene O'Neill, Noel Coward, and Edward Albee. Jill, a lonely only child growing up in a small town, early embraced the public library as her best friend. Frank, too, had been an only child, addicted to the library.

"I'll run out and see if the early morning editions are out yet," Scott said with theatrical nonchalance, the scraping of his chair a discordant note. "There's a newsstand right at the corner."

The conversation at the table became stridently ebullient. The reviews could change the future of everybody concerned with the play. Even Frank Danzig was tense while they waited. What a sensitive man, Jill thought with a surge of friendship.

Frank insisted on another round of strawberry shortcake and coffee while they waited for Scott to return. They were all eating compulsively, Jill guessed, while Frank talked about the culinary talents of Clara, the housekeeper-cook who had been with him for twenty-four years.

Then Scott was striding into the restaurant, folded-back paper clutched in one hand.

"The *Times* says it's a bomb," Scott announced flatly.

"Read the review," Elaine said coldly. "Let's hear it."

They sat tight-faced while Scott read in a monotone. One good bit. "Jill Conrad, as Wendy, was lovely in her off-Broadway debut."

"We won't play tomorrow night," Elaine said as Scott handed her the newspaper. Her eyes were angry. "What's the point?"

"Elaine, your bond covers the salaries," Hal

reminded her guardedly, flinching before the hostility in her eyes. "I mean, the cast hope to have agents down to see them during the week." Even though the play was panned, some of the cast clung tenaciously to this.

"Why should I waste money on ads?" Elaine asked brutally. "We opened and closed tonight. The cast can get their salaries from the bond. There'll be no more performances." She pushed back her chair, said a cold good-night to Frank, and stalked from the restaurant. The others watched with varying degrees of indignation.

"Now what?" Frank asked.

"Now it starts all over again." Jill's voice was deep with distaste. "Working at temporary jobs that pay the rent, making rounds in between. Hoping for another part."

"Not me," Scott said suddenly, and Jill's eyes swung, startled, to his. "I'm cutting out. I've had it in this town. I've got enough salted away to buy a cheap secondhand Volkswagen. I'm heading for California. TV work is all out there now. Why not?" His eyes held Jill's. "Want a ride out to California, Jill? Plenty of room, and I'd love company."

I'd love company. Not "I love you."

"Thanks, no." Jill's smile was strained. "I'd hate California." It was worse out there than it was in New York. But New York was going to be awful without Scott. In four weeks she'd learned to cling to him. Four weeks in rehearsal was like four months of normal living.

"I'm going back up to Maine tomorrow," Frank said quietly to Jill. "If you'd like to come up and stay — as long as you like — we'd be glad to have you." His eyes were strangely eager.

"I — I don't know," Jill stammered. "I'll think about it. And thanks."

But even then, at four in the morning at a table at Ratner's, littered with barely touched plates of strawberry shortcake and half-filled cups of lukewarm coffee, Jill knew she would go to Cliff House.

Chapter Two

Don Munson was scolding his patient and the patient's wife for not calling him earlier, though he knew it was their anxiety about running up a bill that caused this delay. The next-door neighbor dashed importantly into the ill-heated, ramshackle house, just as he picked up his bag to leave.

"Call for Doc Munson," she announced breathlessly. "Knew you were here because I saw your car." Slowly they were losing their distrust of the new young doctor imported by Frank Danzig. "You gonna come take it or you too busy?"

"He'll come," Munson's patient said quickly. There was a glint of gratitude in his eyes because Munson had agreed to make this house call, when the family were patients of old Doc McTavish. But when McTavish went hunting, Don knew, the whole town would have to be dying before he'd come back. "You go on, Doc."

"I'll be back to chew you out some more," Don scolded humorously. Straightening his tall, lean body. Running a hand through his sandy hair, which was rather long for this part of the country. After eight months in town still a stranger among the villagers, he thought wryly, his hazel eyes serious, belying his cordial smile. Called in guardedly by those who were antagonized by the old doctor's cantankerous manner and disregard for their welfare on his "off days," as he approached seventy-six.

The answering service, to whom Don religiously gave an itinerary of his travels, had collected four calls. When they piled up to that point, the girl was under instructions to contact him. She rattled off the calls, winding up with a vague request from Clara, at Cliff House, to give her a call "if he wasn't too busy."

Don returned to his patient to leave final instructions, but made no attempt to collect his fee on the spot, as McTavish was inclined to do. Then he headed for the car. Inside, the windows tightly shut against the March cold, he reached to switch on the heater, enjoying the almost immediate rush of warmth.

He drove down the road to the filling station where there was a pay phone, to follow through on the calls.

"Don't use that phone, Doc," the attendant exhorted as Don strode toward the phone booth, change in hand. "We pay the same bill here no matter how many calls we make on the line."

Don had taken care of a hand infection for the attendant, who had been reluctant to seek medical help, and now he was one of the growing clique of Dr. Don Munson fans.

Don answered his first three calls, decided to

drop by Cliff House instead of calling Clara. Clara was nervous about her mother, though there was never anything different about her condition. She was eighty-three and a hypochondriac. But Don felt a special obligation for the household at Cliff House. He could ease Clara's nervousness, even though he couldn't bring himself to tell her that her mother was an old fraud.

Behind the wheel of his secondhand Fiat, Don remembered the meeting with Frank Danzig that had brought him to the Maine village. Their first encounter had been at a free concert in Central Park. The second was at a performance of an off-Broadway play for which Frank had a pair of tickets. Much later, Don realized that Frank had manipulated that meeting. He'd seemed so gentle, so uncomplicated; but undoubtedly, Don conceded, Frank Danzig was the most complex man he'd ever known.

After the performance Frank had taken him to a restaurant for supper. Their conversation had leaped animatedly from one area to another. Danzig astonished Don with the breadth of his knowledge. His articulate, impassioned urging that Don accept his offer to set him up in practice when he finished his residency in a few weeks was even more surprising.

"No obligations on either side," Frank said, retreating into casualness. "I'll provide the office and equipment. Give it a try for a year. If we're both satisfied, you'll be set with a practice. You can pay off the equipment over a ten-year period." He smiled, almost shyly. "And all that time you'll be enjoying the unspoiled coastline of our section of Maine." Where property owners like Frank were doggedly resisting the offers of resort developers.

Raised as he'd been in a low-income section of Brooklyn, battling his way through college and med school — as his two older sisters had fought their way to teaching degrees — Don was involuntarily skeptical of Frank's simple philanthropy. Yet, he told himself repeatedly, there was much more to Frank Danzig than he revealed to the world.

Now, Don glanced at his watch. He had just about enough time to talk to Clara, have a look at the old lady, and then to stop off to try to persuade Kate Meredith to give a couple of hours twice a day to nursing Mrs. Magnani, a patient who had suffered a stroke. The neighbors meant well, but she needed professional nursing, in part, during these first critical days. And he didn't want to put her through the trauma of a move to the hospital.

Kate kept close to her aunt, Mrs. Webster, only occasionally venturing out socially. But she'd had fifteen years' nursing experience in England until a near nervous breakdown brought her back home, just at the time her elderly aunt failed to the point where it wasn't advisable for her to continue living alone.

Don made a left onto the narrow country road

that would take him to the Victorian house where Frank lived with his housekeeper, Clara, her mother, Jed the houseman, and the group of New York-based guests.

How could a man of Frank's sensitivity bear that ugly monstrosity of a house? But Frank said he'd been living there twenty-four years, ever since he bought the property from Mrs. Webster. It was morbid, the way Mrs. Webster insisted on living in the caretaker's cottage within sight of her daughter's grave, when Denise had been dead for over forty years.

The inside of the house was a happy contrast to the exterior. Frank had spent all these years painstakingly, affectionately, furnishing the house, piece by piece. He was lonely. Frank's face always lit up with pleasure when Don happened to drop by on an evening when there was no immediate demand on his time. How long could a man sit and stare at the Atlantic?

Don drove past the modest caretaker's cottage. Twenty-four years after she'd sold the estate, except for the cottage, Mrs. Webster was still angry at the world because she'd been forced into that sale.

As Don pulled up before the massive house with its slate roof, its multitude of dormers, its endless chimneys, he spied Clara pulling open the heavy oak door to stand before the storm door. She'd heard his car drive up.

"I didn't mean to drag you up here, Dr. Munson," Clara said defensively, thrusting the door open for him. The pleasing aroma of something baking in the oven filled the hall. "I told that girl to just have you phone me if you happened not to be busy."

"I was just down the road a piece," Don explained. "Your mother having problems?" he asked gently. Most of her problems were fears of dying.

"Mama's all right. I'm a little concerned about Mr. Danzig." Her face was etched with anxiety. Clara had gone to school with Frank; but since she'd come to work for him when he bought the house, he'd become Mr. Danzig. "I wish you'd sort of drop by this evenin', the way you do sometimes. He's all stirred up. I worry about him, since that heart attack."

"He can lead a perfectly normal life," Don reminded her gently. "He just has to remember not to overdo."

"I thought maybe he was coming down with a virus." Clara walked down the long corridor toward the kitchen, beckoning him to join her. Clara considered it a breach of good manners to let him leave the house without cake and coffee. "But then it might be that new guest that's comin' up." The hint of agitation in her voice triggered him into alertness. "Some actress he met on his last trip into New York."

"He's always intrigued by his new guests," Don said. Frank's fringe people. Most of them, thus far, with just enough talent to make life anguished.

"This time it's different." A nerve twitched in her eyelid. "You get to know a man, Doc Munson, when you live under the same roof with him for twenty-four years. He's all nerved up."

"Clara, you suspect a romantic attachment?" Don joshed, and was immediately sorry. Clara's faded blue eyes were indignant.

"A man of his age? I'm just scared some of those city folks — you know how they come up here and use him — I'm scared somebody will take him over."

"Clara, he's far too shrewd to be taken over." Then he sniffed appreciatively. "What's that in the oven?"

"Apple turnovers." She was faintly mollified by his interest. "I've got fresh coffee perkin'."

"I've got about ten minutes before I have to get on my rounds," he said.

"Plenty of time. The coffee's been perkin' long enough, and I was just about to take out the turnovers."

Don dropped into a chair at the table by the window. His eyes focused sympathetically on Clara.

"Clara, stop worrying about Frank. No actress from New York is going to turn his head."

"They use him," Clara repeated, tugging at the pan in the oven. "That's what makes me so all-fired mad. They all use him."

Which was the real Frank Danzig? The diffident, reserved man who welcomed strangers into his home with poignant eagerness? Or the astute inventor who had doggedly struggled through the years to build a two-man operation into a successful manufacturing plant employing over a hundred men? A true Yankee horse trader in the business world, yet a man with an astonishing knowledge of theater and the arts.

A complex man, Don decided, with respect.

Chapter Three

Jill sat tense and overwarm in her seat in the sparsely occupied bus. Since she had changed buses at Ogunquit, they had been bound in a depressing, near-freezing March downpour that made the bus an island.

"Good thing it's not five degrees colder," the middle-aged man seated directly behind the driver commented to him. "You'd have six inches of snow before you finish with your run."

"We don't worry too much about snow," the driver said. "They clean these roads pretty quick up here. They have to," he added with a chuckle, "or we'd be in a devil of a mess."

Jill stirred restlessly. Sheila had thought her out of her mind to run up to Frank Danzig's house this way.

"What do you know about him?" Sheila had demanded. "How do you know what you're walking into?"

"Sheila, he's opened his house to strangers, made it a sort of mini-art colony because he's lonely. He loves people who're involved in the arts."

"That's what he says." Sheila stared at her. "How do you know?"

"Oh, Sheila, if you'd spent two hours with Frank, you'd realize the kind of man he is."

At the moment Cliff House seemed to be a sanctuary. She shivered, remembering the sick feeling deep in her stomach, the cold, perspiring hands each time she stood before a casting agent's door and geared herself to walk inside. For a little while she clung to the prospect of making rounds with Scott. But Scott was gone.

Everything was working out well, she told herself with determination. What luck, that Sheila's aunt chose this month to come into New York for out-patient orthopedic treatment. She'd been delighted to move into the apartment and share the expenses for a month instead of going to a hotel.

But now, in the hothouse warmth of the bus, Jill was suddenly cold. Was Sheila right? Was she acting irrationally to rush up to Maine this way, to live for a month in the house of a man she'd met just once?

Jill stared at the sheet of rain outside the window as she tried to consider everything logically. No. She wasn't behaving absurdly. After the play closed with such brutal abruptness — and with Scott running off like that — she knew she must have a chance to regain her perspective. To decide where she was going.

Why had she allowed Scott to become so important in her life in only four weeks? Because she'd been so insecure, so scared. He was brash, warm, charming. And she'd had such respect for his acting ability. Someday he'd make it. Sheila said he was the Hollywood-TV type. He'd probably wind up in a TV series.

Jill had phoned Frank a few nights after the play closed, fearful for a few moments that he wouldn't be back home yet. But he was.

"Come right up," he'd urged gently. "I have only four guests. I'll tell Clara to prepare the other room for you. Call me when you make your travel arrangements. Jed will meet you with the car at the bus station."

She had gone right out to buy the bus ticket. Running. Standing in line before a ticket window in the Port Authority with conflicting emotions. Relief. Anticipation. And creeping apprehension because Sheila still fought her leaving. Even if her aunt moved in, Sheila insisted, they could rent a day bed for the month, squeeze it into the living room.

"It's all those books you read on the job," Jill teased Sheila, who found such pleasure in being a junior editor. "Your imagination keeps riding a roller coaster."

An hour out of Ogunquit the rain changed to a combination of sleet and snow; the sky an ominous gray. The bus suddenly a strange, foreboding vehicle, carrying her into the unknown.

An uneasiness began to trickle through Jill as she tried to visualize Frank Danzig's Victorian house. Remembering that she had promised to remain at least four weeks. She'd never bring herself to break that promise, no matter how much she disliked staying at Cliff House.

The bus lumbered off the highway. From the signs Jill realized they were approaching her destination. The bus turned into what she guessed was the main street of the town. The blend of snow and sleet had petered out now, but ice-laced puddles adorned every indentation in the road. About a dozen small stores lined the two sides of the business block. All of them, except for an unexpectedly contemporary gift shop with a red-and-white-striped awning, had a turn-of-the-century aura.

The bus grunted to a stop before a luncheonette, its plate glass window steamed over, screening off the interior. The "bus stop," Jill decided, and hopped down from the bus to the sidewalk. While she waited for the driver to bring her luggage, her eyes anxiously scanned the scenery for the car that was to be waiting for her.

Three vintage cars sat beside a length of curb. No driver behind the wheel of any of them. Alarm tugged at her. Wasn't she being met? Was there a taxi in town?

She stood uncertainly as the bus churned into motion again, leaving her abandoned. But as the bus pulled away she saw the brilliant blue Bentley that sat at the curb across the street, in front of the barber shop.

The driver was ambling across the slushy street to where she waited with her luggage. She hadn't expected Frank Danzig to own a Bentley.

"You Miss Conrad?" He squinted at her standing in the dreary late afternoon light with something painfully akin to disbelief on his face. Was she so different from the other guests at Cliff House?

"Yes, I am." She forced a smile.

"I'm Jed." He introduced himself with a nasal twang. "You wanna go into Bill's there for a cup of coffee before we drive to the house?" He nodded toward the steamed-over luncheonette window. She suspected Frank had suggested this. "We're a piece from town. About fifteen minutes on these wet roads."

"I had coffee a little while ago," she said. Not entirely truthful. Two hours ago, when the bus had stopped, she'd gone into the diner for a sandwich and coffee, and brought a container of coffee aboard with her to help while away the time. Today she was too restless to read. A strange disquietude plagued her.

She followed Jed to the Bentley, climbed into the rear seat with its elegant white leather upholstery. Relieved that Jed had showed on schedule. Yet she settled herself in one corner with a sense of unreality.

They left the row of stores behind them, moved past blocks of small, modest houses, a white church that hinted at a low-income parish. Then they were moving into the outlying area, with houses more scarce, set acres apart. Power lines stretched along empty swathes of land, utilitarian, unpretty. The winter scenery was stark. Mountains in the distance. The scent of the sea in the air.

Jed cut off onto a narrow, winding dirt road. The trees stood winter-bare against the somber sky. None of the affluence here that she associated with resort Maine. Where was Frank's house? They should be arriving soon.

"House is just a piece ahead," Jed announced, breaking his silence, as though he had read her mind. "Clara'll have coffee waitin' for you." The information was given with reluctance.

"Fine." She struggled to sound enthusiastic, as she leaned forward slightly in her impatience to see Cliff House.

"That's the old caretaker's cottage, near the edge of the road," Jed said, slowing down for a turn. "Mrs. Webster lives there now with her niece. That's the house up there, settin' on the edge of the cliff."

Jill's eyes swept past the caretaker's cottage, up the long driveway lined with towering evergreens. Not at all the kind of house she'd expected. Huge, unappealing. A sprawling verandah spread across the front of the house and around to one side. A small balcony incongruously perched atop the roof, off what appeared to be a group of attic rooms. An architectural afterthought.

"Been standin' there since 1800," Jed said while she inspected the exterior. Lights shone from windows on all three floors against the gloom of the late afternoon. "They don't build houses like that no more. Solid as the Rock of Gibraltar."

"It's huge." She hid her disappointment. She'd expected a charming, much smaller house.

"Mr. Danzig keeps one wing shut off. Still, Clara and me got a dozen rooms to worry about keepin' clean, with a woman in just one day a week to help. Them rooms are pretty well filled up with Mr. Danzig's guests most of the time." An undercurrent of scorn in his voice.

Jill leaned forward to squint with nearsighted curiosity at the "No Hunting" signs tacked about on the spare, gray trees about the property, in such contrast to the stalwart evergreens along the driveway.

"Mr. Danzig don't hold with killin'," Jed contributed. "Not even 'possums."

Now she could see the ornateness of the big house, the curlicued railing that edged the rambling verandah. The chimneys that cut through the roof. She sniffed with sudden delight. The realization that birch logs were burning in a fireplace inside was absurdly reassuring for the moment.

The driveway curved. A car was parked off to one side. Jill's attention focused on a tableau to the far right as Jed maneuvered the curve. A small wrought iron fence enclosed a single gravesite. Within the fence, before the tall, narrow granite tombstone a man rested on his haunches. The magnificent, long-stemmed red roses in his hands seemed exotic in this setting. The man was arranging the red roses in a papier-mâché vase. Involuntarily Jill shivered. In this wet, near-freezing weather every rose would be dead by nightfall.

All at once Jill was conscious that Jed was watching her in the rearview mirror.

"You're the first one ever arrived when *he* was here," he said, inching slowly up the icy driveway.

"Who is he?" Jed was waiting for the question.

"Well now, it's somebody different every year." Garrulous now that he was on home territory, and enjoying this moment of drama, he continued. "For forty years now somebody from a florist shop down in the city comes up here every year on this day, the day she died, just to deliver them red roses to that grave. Them flowers always arrive."

Despite the warmth of the car Jill felt chilled as they moved past the small plot. The roses were all in the vase now, swaying in the wind, the first red petals already dropping to the slush-covered earth. The man rose, reached for the wrappings that had encased the flowers, and headed stolidly for his car.

"Who's buried there?"

"Denise Webster. She was born in this house. Was eighteen when she died. Fell out an attic window. Up there —" He pointed to a dormer.

"How awful," Jill whispered.

Jill was conscious that Jed continued to stare

at her in the rearview mirror. She tried to ignore this. It was stupid to be uncomfortable.

Jed pulled up before the house. Jill reached for the car door. Frank would be at the plant at this hour. She wished wistfully that he were here. But she must walk alone into that awesome house. Meet Clara. Meet the four other guests. *Why had she come?*

"Watch them stairs," Jed cautioned, pulling her two pieces of luggage from the front seat to move gingerly over the ground. "Got patches of ice there."

Why was she so uneasy about going into an unfamiliar house? The guests inside were people who came up here, as she had, to get on an even keel again. Why did she have this persistent feeling that when she walked past that much curlicued door — already opening — her life would never be the same.

"Come inside, Miss Conrad," the small spare older woman ordered, in a tone that was faintly querulous, as she hunched her shoulders against the cold. "I got hot coffee waitin' out in the kitchen, and some of last night's blueberry pie warmin' in the oven. That oughta hold you till supper."

"Sounds marvelous," Jill said with forced enthusiasm. She stopped to scrape her boots on the rubber mat before she walked into the house.

"I'm Clara," the woman at the door introduced herself, and stopped short with shock as Jill stepped into the unexpectedly beautiful foyer. "You look — you're so young!" She was visibly disturbed. "Mr. Danzig never brought up anybody so young before! Whatever will you do with yourself in this dreary place?"

"Well, I love to read." Jill managed a casual smile as her eyes swept about the antique-lined foyer and corridor, noted the exquisite crystal chandelier. "Take long walks along the sea." Why did Clara flinch that way?

"The sea's an ugly thing in winter." Her faded eyes darkened with distaste before she turned to Jed. "Jed, you take them valises up to the room I fixed for Miss Conrad. You come out to the kitchen with me, young lady." Her tone was softer now. Conciliatory. "After all them hours on the bus, you can do with some hot coffee. You can meet the others later." Jill's radar picked up Clara's contempt for "the others."

Jill walked with Clara down the long, narrow, elegantly carpeted corridor, lighted by fine old wall sconces that looked as though they might have been imported from a French palace. The wallpaper was velvet-embossed in muted shades of green, matching the carpeting, an attractive background for the priceless antiques — the whole a dramatic contrast to the exterior of the house.

"In here." Clara invited her into the huge, square kitchen.

A massive round maple dining table, surrounded by captain's chairs with brilliant red cushions, stood in front of a triple small-paned window draped with immaculate, white, criss-cross curtains. Across the room a brick-faced country fireplace, large enough to roast a pig, rose amidst a collection of unexpectedly modern kitchen cabinets, appliances, counter space.

While she poured coffee and brought the blueberry pie from the oven, Clara talked in a dry monotone about Frank's guests. Marian Carlyle, a character actress, had been at Cliff House for three months already. Clara's attitude indicated she considered it time Miss Carlyle returned to the theater.

"Then there's Herb Bronson," Clara continued. "He's a retired bachelor postman who's up here creatin' a life-size sculpture." Her sarcasm was biting. "You'd think he'd freeze to death out in that barn with what little heat he can get from that potbellied stove out there. But out he goes every day to chisel at that chunk of granite. His studio, he calls it."

"Pie's delicious." Jill managed a show of enthusiasm, though she was uncomfortable as Clara ladled out her store of information about the other guests.

"Mel Citron's tryin' to fight off a nervous breakdown," Clara went on, standing at the range before a heavy iron pan inspecting its contents. "He's a bookkeeper by trade, but up here, when he's not paintin', he's writin'." Clara obviously had little patience for Mel Citron's instability.

To Clara, Jill surmised, they were all parasites.

Living on Frank Danzig's largesse. For a woman who must have worked all her life, this would be hackle-raising.

"Clara!" A high-spirited, authoritative, masculine voice echoed down the corridor as its owner approached. "Clara, have you got a cup of coffee for somebody who's been sweating over a hot typewriter all day?"

Along with Clara, Jill swung about to face the new arrival. Tall, massive-shouldered, with unruly ruddy hair and a matching, well-trimmed beard, flashing brown eyes. About thirty, Jill guessed.

"Jason McPherson, do you have to yell loud enough to wake the dead?" But Jill sensed in Clara a furtive admiration for the fourth guest in residence.

"You're Jill Conrad." Jason inspected her with flattering intensity. "What's your scene?"

"I have a degree in drama." Jill shrugged. "Which adds up to nothing."

"Don't knock it," Jason said. "Are you good?" He slid into a chair at right angles to her while Clara bustled off for his coffee. "Frank said he saw you in a play," he recalled now with an air of triumph.

"We opened and closed in one night."

"That doesn't answer my question," he insisted.

"I think I'm good," she said slowly, "when I'm safely in my own pad and not standing under the scrutiny of a producer or a director. It took me nine months to land that one small part in a scruffy production."

"I've been sweating out a book for almost two years. What are you complaining about?" he shot back. "I sit at an office typewriter for six weeks, working through some temporary agency for the bread. Then I cut out and write until my money gives out. I met Frank when I was sunning myself one lean afternoon in Washington Square Park, dreading an imminent return to the temporaries. I thought he was a nut at first when he invited me up here. But here I'll stay until the book's finished. To my satisfaction. And I've promised him," Jason said with a laugh, "that I'll be his first major success."

"Everybody up here thinks they're so special," Clara grumbled, sliding coffee and a generous slice of blueberry pie in front of Jason. "They all got some gift. Lots of talk, but no action."

"I'm selling *this* book, Clara." Jason's eyes were uncompromising. "It's my time, I feel it. I remember some quotation — Shakespeare, I think. 'To everything there is a season —' And mine's coming up."

"It's not Shakespeare," Clara contradicted. "It's from the Bible."

"This is my time." Jason thumped on the table with one clenched fist. Then he considered a moment and leaned forward with a sudden, brilliant smile. "Clara, I'll dedicate my book to you."

"Don't you help yourself to no more of that

42

pie," Clara warned him, pleased, but not fooled by his promise. "I got a Yankee pot roast on the stove. I expect you to make a sizable dent in that at dinner." Then, almost brusquely, she turned to Jill, who was draining her second cup of coffee. "You ready to go up to your room, Miss Conrad?"

"Thank you, yes."

Clara and Jill were halfway down the corridor when a tall, heavy woman in her early fifties emerged from double doors on the right. She wore a dazzling print jersey dress and a lot of costume jewelry. Her hair, worn unbecomingly severe, was a harsh black that undoubtedly acquired its color from a bottle. Her eyes, heavily mascaraed, were a surprising young blue. Once, Jill thought, she must have been an attractive woman. Twenty years younger, sixty pounds lighter.

"You are the young actress Frank met on his last trip into New York," she said with a theatrical flourish. "I am Marian Carlyle. Call me Marian."

"Jill Conrad," she introduced herself. "I was in one off-Broadway play for one performance."

"Was it one of those awful plays where the language is obscene and everybody throws off their clothes?" Marian asked distastefully. Clara looked shocked.

"No, it wasn't," Jill said swiftly.

"The theater is in such a shocking state."

43

Marian sighed. "The theater of the absurd — the theater of the obscene. Where is the beauty that used to be?"

"You can talk about that at dinner," Clara said impatiently. "I gotta see Miss Conrad settled in her room."

For one charged moment Jill looked upon the naked hate that flashed between the two women. Frank Danzig, so gentle, so eager to bring strangers into his home — yet in this house they radiated contempt, anger, even hate.

Clara and Jill climbed the thickly carpeted stairs to the second floor. Clara paused before a door to the far right, pulled it wide.

"Here," she said tersely, and Jill suspected her thoughts were still with Marian Carlyle. "Mr. Danzig wants you in here."

The corner room was delightfully feminine. The furniture an eclectic blend of antiques. The three papered walls adorned with elegant group-ings of beautifully framed miniatures. The fourth wall was paneled, offering a random array of bookshelves, the books adding color to the room. The fireplace, where birch logs were piled in readiness, was faced with green-veined marble that lent an Old World elegance.

"What a lovely canopied bed." Jill's eyes moved admiringly from the bed to the matching drapes at the tall, narrow windows, which she hoped would look out upon the Atlantic.

"He spent a lotta time fixin' up this one." Clara's eyes were enigmatic. "You want any-

thing, just holler. Oh, the bathroom's in there."
She pointed to a door. "Everybody's got their
own."

As Clara closed the door behind her, Jill
crossed to a window, pushed aside the drapes.
Her eyes fastened compulsively on the rocky,
treacherous shore below. What an awful drop!
She shivered, remembering the girl who had
fallen to her death from an attic window, and
imagined the broken body of Denise Webster
sprawled there on the rocks. Feeling the sea
dampness in the room despite the generous heat
from the radiators.

Jill started at the brisk knock at the door,
swung about to call out quickly, "Come in."
Thinking it was Clara with some exhortation
about being down for dinner.

Marian Carlyle strode into the room.

"Do you like the sea, Jill?" An odd monotone
in her voice, as though she were playing a role in
an old-fashioned melodrama, Jill thought.

"I love it," Jill said quickly, brushing aside her
earlier reaction to the treacherous stretch of
shore below her windows. "With the fervor of
someone who's grown up a landlubber."

"I, too, love the sea." Marian smiled, an enig-
matic smile that matched the secrecy of her eyes.
"I stand on the rocks and the sea talks to me.
Clara thinks I'm daffy, but *the sea talks to me.*"
She gripped her hands together in agitation,
frowned heavily. "Jill, don't stay here at Cliff
House. Don't stay in this town. The sea tells me.

45

This is a dangerous place for you. Stay and something terrible will happen."

Jill stared in shock.

"I'm sure nothing will happen to me here, Miss Carlyle," she protested gently, ". . . Marian. Besides, I've promised Frank I'd stay at least four weeks. I couldn't walk out on a commitment."

Marian gazed at her with ill-concealed rage.

"There is no commitment when your life is at stake. I have told you, Jill. The sea cries out to you. Go! Go now! Tonight."

And then Marian Carlyle, with an unexpected grace considering her bulk, exited as she might have from a Broadway stage.

Marian was playing a role, Jill told herself. She lived between the pages of a playscript. But Jill's heart thumped as she heard the angry waves pounding at the rocky coastline below, and she recalled the rage in Marian Carlyle.

Marian's warning was only a ruse to drive her from Cliff House. *Why* was it so important to Marian Carlyle that she leave?

Chapter Four

Frank sat behind the oversized desk in his rather small office, which only in the last year had been attractively wood-paneled and carpeted. He shuffled through the papers in the folder before him, then spoke to his efficient, middle-aged secretary, who had been taking dictation.

"That's all for today, Mattie. You can type them up tomorrow."

"You want some coffee before I leave, Mr. Danzig?" she asked solicitously, though he knew she was anxious to get home to start supper preparations for her family.

"Thank you, no, Mattie."

He waited, with concealed impatience, for her to leave the office, to close the door behind her. Then he reached for the phone. Dialed. A quiver in his eyelid gave testimony to his tension.

"Hello." Clara answered with that querulous tone that indicated whoever was calling was interrupting a chore. Frank guessed she was upset because of Jill. He'd expected that. She was anxious about anything that might agitate him. She couldn't accept Don's verdict that his health was fine now.

"Did she arrive?" Frank asked briskly. He

always called about each guest this way, he reminded himself guiltily.

"She's here. Jed picked her up. The bus was right on time." There was anxiety in her voice despite her effort to mask it, but she couldn't bring herself to say what was really on her mind. "Mr. Danzig, what's a young girl like that gonna do with herself all day in this big old house?"

"She'll rest, relax, and eat your terrific meals." He ignored Clara's grunt. "Probably put on ten pounds before the month is out." She wasn't going to say anything else about Jill, he decided with relief.

"Pot roast for dinner," Clara said. "I'd like to take it out by seven."

"I'll be there," he promised, and put down the phone.

Frank pushed down an eagerness to leave the office right now. That would be giving away his anxiety to get home, to see Jill Conrad installed at Cliff House. This must seem just another, normal day.

He swung around in his swivel chair, inspected the beginning snowfall. Better snow than sleet. Less depressing. This time of year he always fought depression. Last year hadn't been as bad as usual because of the guests in the house. And this month lovely, bright Jill Conrad would be in residence. As he'd sat in that tiny, darkened theater, watching her move with grace about the stage, he'd known he wouldn't rest until he had persuaded her to

48

come to Cliff House.

He killed another hour going over accounts, then reached for his coat and headed out of the building toward the parking area.

"Good-night, Jim," he called to the night watchman. Waving a hand in farewell.

In the heavily falling snow he walked to the dark blue Mercedes, climbed behind the wheel, drove out onto the road. The sanders were out already, he noted with approval. With the sharp drop in temperature and the heavy sky, they might be in for eight or ten inches.

Ten minutes later Frank turned into his private driveway, already white with snow. His eyes swung to the single gravesite. All day long, at odd intervals, he'd thought about the red roses that would be there today.

Tonight, for the first time in years, he was conscious of the ugliness of the house. But it had been enough to change the interior, slowly, laboriously. He thought, with intense satisfaction, not a house in the county could touch it — once you got past the front door.

Frank checked his watch as he left the car for Jed to take around to the garage for him, and walked up to the verandah. Seven sharp. The downstairs library was brilliantly lighted. The others would be gathered there, waiting for Clara to announce dinner. His temporary family.

He hung his slightly damp coat on a hook outside the closet, installed at Clara's instructions years ago for just such weather. Now he walked straight down the corridor to the library. Hearing the jumble of voices. Jill's light, musical voice in earnest discussion with Jason.

At the door he paused, not yet seen by the others. His footsteps had been cushioned by the lush carpeting in the corridor. There she stood, fragile and lovely, her eyes aglow as she argued with Jason, who was probably deliberately baiting her with that fey sense of humor of his. Mel in a chair, reading a newspaper. Angry at the political picture, at the inequities of the world, as usual. Marian and Herb in quiet conversation. Marian's eyes moving covertly to Jill, who was so young.

"Welcome to Cliff House, Jill," he said, and suddenly the atmosphere in the room was tense. Silently they all turned to him. Each new arrival was a star for the moment, and the others felt fleetingly rejected. "I hope you'll enjoy being here."

"Thank you," Jill said softly. "I've never seen such a magnificently furnished house. I'm almost afraid to touch anything."

"Everything in this house was chosen to be lived with," Frank said with conviction. "It's my pleasure to see you enjoy it all."

"Supper," Clara announced sourly from the doorway. "Come and get it while it's hot."

They moved into what Frank called the family dining room. It was a replica, from the Louis XV chandelier, the Queen Anne candlesticks, to the authentic Windsor chairs, of an old country manor house dining room he had seen in Suffolk, England, on one of his rare trips to Europe. He had been enchanted, each time he traveled abroad, with the richness of tradition about him; but his loneliness was only intensified. In New York he communicated with people; he felt he belonged.

"What a marvelous room," Jill looked around in admiration.

Despite its old European air — Frank had added the massive oak beams, brick-faced the large fireplace, about which hung his collection of Spode — the room belonged in New England, Frank felt sure. He enjoyed Jill's vocal enthusiasm.

They sat themselves around the table, Jill at Frank's left, Jason at his right. Marian installed, as usual, at the opposite end of the table, appointing herself Cliff House's hostess. Herb and Mel flanked Marian.

"Nobody cares about what talents you have," Mel was grumbling. "They throw you into a job and you're supposed to rot there for the rest of your life."

"I've managed to survive in the theater," Marian contradicted with pride, but she turned her head quickly to Frank. Frank knew how Marian survived. On unemployment, and temporary jobs when that ran out, until the next tiny character role arrived.

Jed, who had at first balked at helping with the

51

serving, arrived with a steaming tureen of vege-
table soup, which Marian majestically served as
they passed their plates to her.

Listening to Marian talk at length about a road
tour with a Broadway star seven years ago, in
which she'd played a painfully minor role, Frank
observed his choice of guests with an honesty he
didn't normally permit himself.

Jason, he believed, would make it one day,
right up to the top. But Marian, Mel, and Herb,
and all the others these past months? Was he
doing wrong by them, to give them these weeks
of play-acting? Did they return to their empty
lives with anything more than rested bodies?

Mel was having his lone fling at expressing
himself creatively on a full-time basis. Then he
must return to his petulant wife and the three
teenage kids, none of whom shared — or understood — his creative leanings. Herb would not
be able to take that massive concoction he was
sculpting out in the barn into his bedroom in
Brooklyn. Did they hate him afterward, for
showing them a few weeks of a life at all other
times denied them? For the first time he ques-
tioned his judgment.

"Oh, no, you're wrong." The strident quality
of Marian's voice punctured his introspection.
"Eugene O'Neill won the Nobel prize for litera-
ture, but he didn't win four Pulitzer prizes.
You're both wrong," she was insisting to Jill.
"Frank, you're the O'Neill authority." She
turned to him with a touch of coquettishness

that was incongruous with her *grande dame* manner. "Tell us, did O'Neill win four Pulitzer prizes?"

"I believe he did, Marian," Frank said gently. Marian hated being wrong. She was staring at Jill as though she were angry enough to kill her. "I remember going down to New York to see his 'Long Day's Journey into Night,' " Frank continued. "That was one of the great evenings in theater. That I store along with the night I saw Noel Coward together with the Lunts on Dick Cavett's TV program." His eyes glowed with nostalgia. "I wished I could have taped that."

"I saw that show!" Jill glowed. "Weren't they marvelous? Of course, I had a miserable time getting up next morning. I had to be at my temporary typing assignment at nine sharp."

Frank felt the resentment of the others when Jill brought her prosaic typing job into the conversation. Again he wondered, was he wrong in giving them these weeks at dabbling in the arts? But Mel, in a moment of quiet truth, had told him that without these weeks at Cliff House he would have had a nervous breakdown.

"This is a kind of anniversary for me," Frank said slowly. Clara, who had come in with the platter of sliced pot roast, stared sharply at him. "Thirty years ago today my novel was published." Why had he said that? It had slipped out because he was keyed up tonight. He never mentioned it to anybody. Yet there was this compulsion in him now to speak about it.

"Frank, you wrote a novel?" Jason inspected him with a mixture of disbelief and curiosity.

"Oh, it never got off the ground." His hands were trembling as he tried to cut his pot roast. Why hadn't he kept his mouth shut? It was a closed era in his life.

Thirty years closed.

"First novels rarely sell well," Jill said. "I've heard my roommate say that dozens of times." Her eyes, too, were bright with curiosity. "You didn't just stop writing?"

"I stopped writing," Frank said. Remembering how he'd arrived at that anguished decision all those years ago. "I put four years of my life into that book. There was no time for anything else. It took me two years to sell it. Another year for it to come out." He forced himself to look at Jill. "That was it."

"But you shouldn't have stopped writing!" Jill protested. She was upset, Frank thought — the young were so vulnerable. No, that was wrong. The creative were vulnerable. "Frank, why didn't you write other books?"

"I buried myself in business," he admitted. "I invented this silly tool, and I realized it filled a need. I could build it into a financially rewarding business." He gestured futilely.

"What did it cost you to bring out the book, Frank?" Jason asked sympathetically.

"It wasn't a vanity publication," Frank shot back with pride. More sharply than he intended. He named his publisher, and Jason pantomimed respect. The others were staring at Frank as though he had six heads and green hair.

"Why didn't you ever tell us?" There was hostility in Herb's voice. "You let us believe you were just a — a tool manufacturer."

"So I wrote a book." Frank shrugged. His eyes moved about the table. "It sold eleven hundred copies." To the others this was success. He had been published. He was no longer a fan. He was, in some absurd fashion, competition.

"May I read it?" Jill asked. "Please?"

"I'll get a copy out of the barn storeroom one of these days," he promised. "If you really want to read it?" Why did he feel this eagerness to acquire another reader, after all these years?

"Oh, Frank, I do!" Jill smiled brilliantly.

"You couldn't have been deeply attuned to writing," Jason said, "or you would have written despite the sales figures." He was intrigued by this new side of Frank.

"I write at night and on weekends," Mel said sternly. "I spent my whole last vacation working on a short story." His eyes were somber. Antagonistic. "When you have a talent, how can you deny it?"

"I couldn't afford another four years of working on a book," Frank said. Jason had him pegged for a four-year dilettante, but he had had a novel published. Jason's back was up. If he were Jason's age again, would he manage his life differently? Would he have fulfilled himself? "My parents were both ill at the time," he forced himself to elaborate. "I had to take over my father's small store. After they died, within three months of each other, I sold the business and went into manufacturing. I started with a workshop that was twelve by fifteen. With one man helping me."

"So beneath that gentleness, Frank," Jason said with friendly raillery, "there's a hardheaded, driving business man. You made it in your own field. Don't sell yourself short."

But he had wanted to write, Frank admitted on this the thirtieth anniversary of his first grasp at success. But all the books after the first one had been aborted. He had only the boxes and boxes of notes he'd kept through the years. Suddenly he felt very tired. Very old.

Chapter Five

Jill was relieved when Jason deftly turned the conversation away from Frank's novel. It was easy to launch Marian on a flood of theatrical reminiscences again. Jill concentrated on her food, hearing little of what Marian said, though she managed a facade of lively interest.

Outside the waves churned at the coastline and snow plummeted to earth as though determined to cover every inch in record time. What was it Marian said about the sea? "The sea talks to me."

Jill would *not* be unnerved by that absurd warning. It was ridiculous to keep thinking about it at unwary moments this way. Marian lived in a strange world of her own. Who would want to hurt Jill in this small Maine town? Nobody even knew her. Yet she felt a certain amount of hostility from Frank's guests. As though she were a threat to their status.

"Frank, what's the story about that grave on the property?" Jason suddenly asked. Jill saw Frank flinch, but Jason went on, "Clara was very evasive when I asked about the man with the red roses."

Frank whitened.

"Clara told you all there is to tell." He put down his fork abruptly and leaned forward to gaze toward the doorway. "Clara," he called out with rare brusqueness, "we'll have dessert and coffee in the library. And make sure Jed has the fire started."

Clara appeared in the doorway, her eyes reproachful.

"Jed always starts the fire soon as you sit down to dinner," she reminded him. "And I'll bring dessert and coffee into the library as soon's everybody's finished here." The faint reproof in her voice was directed at Jason and Herb, who were still eating.

"I'm sorry." Frank turned to Jason, then to Herb, upset that he'd spoken harshly. "Please don't rush."

Frank was bitter beneath that gentle demeanor, Jill suddenly decided. Gentleness was a penalty he demanded of himself for failing. Thirty years later he was still angry about all the other books he hadn't written because of that first anguished rejection. How desperately hurt he must have been. Perhaps it just hadn't been his time. Ten years later, or twenty years later, the book might have been well received.

The doorbell rang and Jed hurried down the corridor to answer. The scent of birch logs could be sniffed in the dining room. Jill heard the crackle of the logs in the fireplace. Such a delightful sound.

At the door Jed was talking to someone.

Frank's face brightened in recognition of the voice.

"That's Don Munson, our new doctor," he said with pleasure. "You'll like him, Jill."

"Oh, yes, Dr. Galahad," Jason drawled. Jill recognized the note of hostility in his voice. Jason was so driven to admire success, that he felt only contempt for a young doctor who would bury himself in a small town, especially in this era when practically every doctor in the nation had an impressive income.

"Don Munson," Frank said with a kind of pride, "is one of that rare breed of doctors, the kind we used to have forty or fifty years ago. He doesn't flinch at making house calls. He charges what his patients can afford. He's concerned."

They heard Jed and the new arrival talking in the corridor as the doctor shed his coat and boots. Jed was taking him to the library. In a moment Jed appeared in the doorway.

"Doc Munson's here," Jed reported and broke into a big smile. "I told him he was just in time for dessert and coffee." Jed's grin showed a need for dental work. "He never minds that."

The others left the table to go into the library. Except for her, Jill realized, they all knew Don Munson. Except for Jason, they all obviously liked him.

Frank fell into step beside Jill. Marian was talking animatedly to Herb, but she managed to stare over her shoulder at Frank and Jill. Nettled by Frank's attentions to Jill. Poor Marian, Jill

59

thought sympathetically. All that show of confidence, almost of arrogance, but underneath she was afraid because the years were running away and she was alone. Making the rounds of agents, Jill had met so many Marian Carlyles in their waiting rooms.

The library was a surprisingly modern room, for a house filled with authentic antiques. Three walls book-lined, the fourth paneled and glowing with care. The wall-to-wall beige carpeting emphasized the stillness of the house. The furniture, including a sprinkling of smart, comfortable chairs and a large sofa — upholstered in black leather with colorful cushions — was contemporary. A massive oak coffee table with shelves beneath for books, was strategically placed. What beautiful drapes, Jill thought, staring at the crimson splash of color at the windows, falling impressively from ceiling to floor.

Don Munson stood by the fireplace, warming his hands. He looked up with a wide smile as they walked into the library. And then his eyes settled on Jill, and lingered with disconcerting intensity.

"Jill, this is Don Munson," Frank introduced. "After me, he's Clara's number one fan. Jill Conrad, Don. She just arrived this afternoon."

"The weather was not cooperative," Don said in a low, pleasant voice that would be most reassuring to patients, she guessed. "I'm sure Frank ordered a spring-like day." He turned to Frank, reluctant to remove his eyes from Jill. "I had to be at the cottage." Frank's eyebrows rose questioningly. "No, Mrs. Webster's fine. I stopped by to persuade Kate to look in on Mrs. Magnani a couple of times a day." His eyes returned to Jill. "She's an elderly patient who just suffered a stroke. I'm trying to keep her at home instead of in the hospital — she'd be terrified in strange surroundings."

A compassionate doctor, Jill thought with respect. Like the others, she felt a spontaneous warmth for Don Munson, whose eyes moved compulsively to Jill even while he talked to the others.

They seated themselves about the room while Clara came in with a tray of dessert plates and silver. Apple pie, Jill noted, and tensed. She'd have to tell Clara she was allergic to the cinnamon in the pie.

"None for me, thank you," she said with a smile of apology. "I'm wildly allergic to cinnamon. It can make me very ill."

Clara stared sharply for a moment.

"I'll bring you some cookies," she said grudgingly.

Jill sat back on the comfortable sofa, between Jason and Frank, with Don installed in a lounge chair at right angles to the sofa. Conscious again of the hammering of the waves against the rocks below. Of the pleasant quietness that pervaded the house. It was as though they were removed from civilization. Except for the cottage below, there wasn't another house in sight. Only vast stretches of land. And the currently turbulent Atlantic.

Clara sent Jed in with the coffee urn and a plate of cookies for Jill. Marian poured. Frank was talking with civic pride about the expansion of the hospital, for which he had campaigned heavily. And to which he'd contributed, Jill surmised, though she was listening only at the periphery of her mind. Feeling, again and again, the weight of Don's eyes on her. Jason noticed, and was amused. At odd intervals she intercepted Marian's somber glances in her direction. Was Marian honestly disturbed about that imagined "voice of the sea"?

Don left early, explaining that he started his rounds at the hospital at seven in the morning. Not long after, Jill, exhausted from her early rendezvous with the bus, began to yawn. Immediately Frank ordered her off to bed. Marian, Herb, and Mel were playing gin. Jason was occupied with the *New York Times*, which Frank received daily by mail.

"I'll be calling it a night soon, too," Frank soothed. "I leave for the plant before anybody else stirs from bed. You sleep late, too, Jill," he urged, because Mel bridled at this reference to an indolent habit.

"Good-night." Jill rose with a smile that encompassed the group.

"Sleep well." Despite the tranquility in Frank's voice, Jill observed the distraction in his

62

"Going somewhere?" Marian inquired brightly from the doorway, coming in for one of her morning coffee breaks.

"I'm picking up Frank for lunch." She was discomforted by Marian's piercing stare. Shouldn't she have mentioned this? "Afterward, I'll be driving into town. Would you like me to bring you anything?"

"Thank you, no." Marian's eyes clouded. Her mouth wore a tight little smile. "Drive carefully. The roads must be a mess."

"Frank said they're cleaned immediately." Marian was annoyed that Jill was meeting Frank for lunch. How absurd! "But thank you," she forced herself into politeness. "I'll be careful, anyway."

In knee-high boots and car coat, Jill left by the kitchen door, which was a short-cut to the garage, Jed explained. He had shoveled a foot-path that way. He had also warmed up the Mercedes in preparation for her jaunt.

Jill slid behind the wheel with an air of anticipation. It felt good to be driving again. She moved cautiously down the long driveway, braking gently at the curve just before the small cottage. A woman was climbing into a vintage Ford that sat beneath the carport. Another woman, considerably older, wrapped up for the weather, was tossing breadcrumbs onto the snow for the birds.

"Good-morning," Jill called out, waving as she inched slowly over the wet curve.

eyes. All that talk about his book.

She was out in the foyer about to mount the stairs when Frank's voice stopped her again. An urgency in his voice that rang bells in her head.

"Jill —" He paused and glanced down the corridor as though uneasy about the others overhearing. "Do you drive?"

"Yes."

"Ask Jed to give you the keys to the Mercedes tomorrow. He has a pick-up truck if he needs to go anywhere. Drop by the plant and pick me up for lunch. I'll show you the town. Unless," he added solicitously, "you'd rather just rest tomorrow?"

"I'd love to have lunch with you," Jill said. "And afterward, if it's all right, I'll drive around a bit. If the roads aren't too bad."

"They make a habit of getting the sanders out fast." Frank smiled. "One of the civic improvements I worked to help bring about." From the grimness in his eyes Jill guessed he'd made enemies on that project. But then, Frank Danzig wasn't all male Pollyanna. He hadn't built a two-man tool business into a plant that employed over a hundred men without being sharp in the business world.

"About twelve?" Jill asked.

"Fine. Good-night, Jill."

She went upstairs to her bedroom, pleased to discover Jed had lighted the fire sometime during the course of the evening. The logs would lend a friendly, ruddy glow far into the night.

She prepared for bed, in her mind comparing Jason and Don. How utterly unlike they were, yet both possessed the same compelling charm. Jason, somehow, made her feel defensive. Still, she was drawn to that vein of iron she felt in him. Jason would make it to the top, and not be too concerned if he trampled someone getting there. Don would allow compassion to get in the way of financial success.

In robe and pajamas, stifling a yawn, she crossed to a window to see if the snow was still falling. Self-consciously avoiding the pair of windows that looked down upon the sea, she thrust aside the drapes at the front.

She gazed out into the darkness. The snow had stopped. A sliver of silver moon was pushing its way from behind the clouds shining on the whiteness everywhere. The evergreens that lined the driveway were heavy with snow. And then her eyes stopped roaming to fasten on the figure at the solitary grave below.

Frank stood at the iron railing, in overcoat and boots, hatless. He looked down at the shattered roses, their petals strewn about the snow like huge droplets of blood. Suddenly she felt herself an intruder and stepped away from the window. Drew the drapes tight. Hurried to the bed.

Jill slept almost until noon and was shocked when she realized the lateness of the hour. She would have just enough time to dress, ask directions to the plant, and drive over to pick up Frank. A gloriously sunny day, belying the bitter cold outdoors.

At Clara's insistence she sat down in the kitchen for a cup of coffee while Jed gave her instructions about reaching the plant.

"You can't miss it. It's just a quarter mile after that left turn," he assured her. But he disapproved of her having lunch with Frank.

In the late morning stillness in the kitchen, they could hear the sound of Herb's hammering in the barn behind the house. The clatter of Jason's typewriter sounded erratically. Mel, Clara reported caustically, was out walking along the shore. Enjoying the quiet while he could, Jill guessed. He had described the raucous apartment battling of his three teenagers. The muted sound of television, emanating from the sitting room off the foyer, told her that Marian was absorbed in some interview show.

"Here're the keys. You ever drive one of them foreign cars?" Jed inquired with skepticism. He considered it a personal affront that Frank was entrusting the Mercedes to her care.

"My father always bought foreign cars." Not strictly true. The last car he'd bought before she went away to college had been a foreign job which they'd chosen together in Sweden on the three-week tour they'd taken as her high school graduation present. For a moment she felt a rush of homesickness. "I won't have any trouble with the car," she promised, rising to her feet.

64
65

The older woman stared hard as Jill passed within three yards of her. Forgetting to feed the birds. Not bothering to acknowledge the greeting.

"Kate!" the older woman called shrilly. "Kate, come here!"

Jill moved out onto the narrow, dirt road, sniffed the salty sea air. The ocean lay to her far right, hidden by the ragged cliffs that edged the property. A view that both intrigued and frightened her.

Frank's plant, a low, sprawling building with its several additions testimony to the growth of the business, lay at the edge of town. When Jill walked into the reception room, his secretary — alerted for her arrival — showed her right into Frank's office. Jill was conscious of stares from the staff. It wasn't often, she surmised, that Frank took someone out to lunch.

"I'll just be a moment, Jill." Frank interrupted his telephone conversation to wave her to a chair.

In five minutes Frank, faintly self-conscious, was guiding her through the offices to the Bentley.

"It's not a New York type of restaurant," he warned with a chuckle, "but it's the only restaurant in town except for Bill's, and you only go there for coffee and a sandwich. But Minnie is an artist with down-to-earth New England Food."

The restaurant, Minnie's Tea Room, was the lower floor of a small, white Revolutionary-

67

period house, set close to the edge of the road. In small rooms off the corridor were tables set for special parties. A large room at the rear served regular luncheon patrons. Tiny kerosene lamps sat on each table, few of which were occupied as yet. But the aroma from the kitchen was appealing.

Frank and Jill sat down, consulted the menus presented by a waitress who welcomed Frank as a "regular." A glint of interest in her eyes because today he wasn't alone.

"The shrimp casserole?" Frank suggested. "You won't be sorry."

Over lunch, as appetizing as Frank had promised, Jill reminded him that he'd promised to let her read his novel.

"I'm always peeking into the manuscripts Sheila brings home. I'm a compulsive reader. I even read bottle labels."

"I'll dig out a copy for you," he said earnestly, after a moment's hesitation. This time she felt he meant it. "Remember, I wrote it thirty years ago." She sensed that his eagerness was mixed with apprehension that she might find it unworthy.

"Have you read anything of Jason's?" she asked curiously.

"No. He won't allow anybody to read the book until it's finished. And he said everything he has done before is garbage." Frank's smile was compassionate. "He's on the home stretch with this one now."

"He talks beautifully about writing," Jill observed. "But I know a lot of actors who talk marvelously about acting," she stared somberly into space, visualizing those brash, confident people who intimidated her, "until they get up to read, and then they're awful."

"I'm betting on Jason to be the real thing," Frank said quietly. "And he's got the drive, which I didn't have. He sits down at the typewriter and he works. I sit in a lounge chair every night, staring into the fire or out at the sea, and I weave stories in my head."

"Why don't you write them down?" Jill leaned forward.

"No more." Frank shook his head. "Just endless notes. Cartons of them."

They finished lunch, lingered briefly over a second cup of coffee, talking about playwrights until a call came from Frank's office to say his afternoon appointment, driving up from Boston, had arrived early.

"I'd planned on showing you around," Frank apologized. "Not that there's much to show."

"That's all right," Jill said quickly. "I'll drive into town, park, and stroll about awhile."

"You won't walk too much in this weather," Frank warned her with a chuckle. "Stop in at Bill's and have coffee before you drive home."

Frank drove her back to the plant, where she picked up the Mercedes for the short drive to Main Street. She parked, lifted the collar of her car coat against the rising wind, dug her gloves from her purse and pulled them on.

She was immediately attracted to the contemporary gift shop with its gay, candy-striped awning, so unlike the other stores along Main Street.

The owner, Chuck Travers, self-exiled from New York since the Joe McCarthy witchhunt days in the early '50s, greeted her with pleasure. He talked about the period that had sent him to Maine to open this small shop.

"I'll never go back to New York," he admitted, "but I enjoy hearing about the city. Frank comes in and talks to me. Tells me what's going on down there each time he comes back from a trip. You *are* Frank Danzig's new guest, aren't you?" His eyes rested speculatively on her.

"Yes." She was faintly uncomfortable. What did a sophisticated man like Chuck Travers think about Frank's guests? That they were a bunch of misfits? No. He was too compassionate, she decided. He'd understand.

"Don't let folks here in town throw you," Chuck warned. "This is a very insular area. They don't welcome strangers too readily."

From Chuck Travers she bought a hand-painted tile to send back to Sheila for the apartment, then went to the general store next door in search of postcards.

What a contrast to Chuck Travers' attractive, cheerful shop! The walls and ceiling drab, stained. The merchandise displayed unappealingly. The proprietor — a tall, potbellied man

with bushy eyebrows and a pugnacious stare —
was arguing with a pair of workmen who'd wandered in to buy shoelaces.

"Sure I'm runnin' for mayor next term," the
man was saying loudly. "You need somebody in
this town who ain't afraid to speak his mind. I
get in, we'll see some cleanin' up around here."

"You'll be cleaning up, Ralph," one of the
workmen jeered. "There won't be a bulldozer
working around here that don't belong to you."

"You lookin' for somethin', Miss?" There was
an odd belligerence in his voice that brought
Jill's back up.

"Postcards." What an obnoxious man!

"Two aisles over. You just passin' through
town?" he asked. The two workmen inspected
her with lively interest.

"I'm staying at Cliff House." Her instinct was
to tell him it was none of his business.

"Oh. Another one of them." Disapproval
laced his voice.

"Getting younger," one of the workmen noted
with approval.

"Postcards two aisles over," the proprietor
pointed. "Pick out what you want and bring 'em
over to the register."

Color staining her cheeks, Jill sought out the
postcards. Chuck Travers had warned her this
was an insular town. Well, the owner of the general store was certainly obvious about his dislike
of Frank's guests.

She chose her postcards quickly, impatient to

71

be out of the store. Digging into her purse for coins, she hurriedly approached the cash register so as not to stay any longer than necessary within these hostile walls.

The cold rushed to encircle her as she left the store. Bitter, biting cold. Now she remembered Frank's exhortation to stop in for coffee before she drove home. Bill's was two doors down. Its window was steamed over, as it had been when she arrived yesterday afternoon.

She reached for the door, pulled it wide, welcoming the warmth that surged forward to greet her. Several electric linemen sat on stools at the counter, kibitzing with the waitress. The tables were deserted.

"Come on, Flo, bring us another cup of that mud," one of the men teased the heavy, elaborately coiffed blonde behind the counter.

Jill moved past the men and climbed on a stool at the end of the counter. A man — tall, gaunt, sixtyish — emerged from the rear with a stack of plates. He set them down, stared hard at Jill, crossed to wipe the counter in front of her.

"Just coffee, please." She was disconcerted by his stare.

"Bring her coffee, Bill," a lineman ordered jovially. "You heard the young lady."

"Just passin' through?" Bill reached for the pot of coffee.

"No." What was the matter with these people? "I'm staying at Cliff House." *That* didn't set well with him. Was everyone who stayed at Cliff

72

House supposed to be some kind of freak?

Jill concentrated on dumping sugar into her coffee. Bill busied himself behind the counter. Almost as though to avoid further conversation with her, Jill thought. But why did he keep shooting those furtive, perturbed glances at her?

Jill finished her coffee, paid her check, and went out into the cold again. The car was quickly warm inside once she switched on the heater. She drove slowly, willing herself to enjoy the austere beauty on display. Back in New York, with this much snow, the streets would be a mess of dirt-tainted slush. Traffic in a snarl.

A stray mutt paused to inspect her as she turned off the road into the driveway. Nobody leashed their dogs here, of course. She called out blithely to him. He barked, tail wagging.

Twenty feet up the driveway the car stalled. Anxiously she pumped the gas pedal. Had she flooded it? Wait a moment. Try again. But another attempt to start the car was futile. She'd have to walk up to the house and ask Jed to come down and take a look at it.

She trudged up the driveway, spied the vintage Ford back in place again. As she moved slowly past the cottage, she could hear the elderly woman inside talking loud enough to be heard in the country quietness.

"Kate, you saw her! Why did he bring that girl here? What is he trying to do?"

Jill's shoulders tensed. Automatically her steps quickened. The old lady was talking about her.

73

About Frank bringing her here. *What did she mean?*

Jill went to the house via the rear path Jed had cleared. He was in the kitchen, piling logs beside the fireplace. She told him about the car's stalling, gave him the keys.

"I'll go take a look at it," he said with a sigh. "Probably flooded it."

Jed reached for a coat, headed out the kitchen door. Jill walked down the corridor. The others were still in the dining room, finishing their rather late lunch. Clara was sullenly serving them coffee.

"Jill," Jason called out. "Come have coffee with us."

"I just did," she said with a smile. "In town. Wow, it's cold!"

"It's the dampness from the ocean," Marian said. "There's this awful feeling of wetness everywhere. Eerie, sometimes, to reach out to touch something and find it damp."

"Marian, you've played in too many melodramas," Jason mocked, and she stiffened defensively.

"I defy anyone to say that this part of Maine isn't damp." Her eyes were coals of anger.

"But it's beautiful." Jason turned on his persuasive charm. "You know it is, Marian."

"In a terrifying way," she acknowledged. Her eyes moved now to Jill. "The sea talks to me. It says such frightening things."

"I'm going upstairs to change," Jill said

uneasily. Why didn't Marian stop this absurd business about the sea? Nothing was going to happen to her at Cliff House.

When Jill was halfway up the stairs a door opened on the second floor. A small, wiry woman pulling a vacuum cleaner emerged. The woman who came in to help with the cleaning, Jill guessed.

The woman was looking for a wall plug in the hall. She found it plugged in the cord, began to vacuum. Not hearing Jill, because of the raucous noise of the appliance, she nearly bumped into her. The woman stared, eyes wide with shock. She crossed herself unconsciously while Jill forced a smile.

"Hello. I'm Jill." Why did the woman cross herself? Why was she so distraught?

"I'm Hallie," the woman said tersely, and deliberately turned her back on Jill to concentrate on the vacuuming.

Bill at the luncheonette. The old lady in the cottage. And now Hallie. *Why did she upset these people?*

Chapter Six

Jason sprawled comfortably in the lounge chair in the small sitting room off the foyer, where the others made a point of gathering in the late afternoon. Usually he went for a walk along the beach about this time. Today he'd been drawn into the group by his writer's curiosity.

They were all worked up because of Frank's admission a couple of nights ago that he had written a book. Before that, Frank was the fan and they were the talents. Their egos had suffered a wrench. They felt threatened.

Of course, publishing was different thirty years ago. It wasn't the hassle it is today. Publishers could afford to take a chance on a new writer. They'd nurture a possible talent. Today you had to come in with something that smelled of the best-seller list, or they were leery.

Frank had told Jason he could stay as long as he needed to finish the book. He wasn't as far along as he intimated, Jason acknowledged somberly. He needed another four or five months. Would Frank buy that? Hell, Frank said he'd spent four years on his book.

"I'm going to rent myself a room when I get back home," Mel was saying with his usual belligerence. "Away from the apartment. I'll go there two or three nights a week and a good chunk of the weekend. Where I can work away from the kids' fighting and my wife's breaking in every ten minutes with some nutty question. It's going to be different," Mel said firmly.

Mel wouldn't rent a room. He couldn't afford it at the price of New York real estate. He'd go on being angry at the world, battling with his wife and kids. Some people could write at night and weekends and publish, Jason knew — not he. Not Mel. But Mel was a rank amateur.

For Jason writing had to be a full-time operation. He couldn't cut himself up in little pieces. Frank would see him through these next five months, wouldn't he? He'd been here over two, with no hints of his wearing out his welcome. The old girl, Marian, had been here three months. What was that crack Jed made the other night, about house-cleaning every four months? An old New England custom, or was it a hint that Frank liked a turnover every four months?

"Somebody's coming," Marian broke off in the midst of a sentence to announce. "I hear a car."

"It's probably the girl," Mel said impatiently. "She went into town again to buy something for Clara."

"I thought it might be Phyllis Lattimer, Frank's friend who is active in local theater. Frank said she had something to talk to me about." With an air of expectancy about her, she

77

listened for further sounds of arrival.

Jill was a looker. Dr. Galahad thought so, too, Jason recalled with amusement. Good-looking enough to stir up even old Frank. Maybe he'd coax her to take a walk along the beach with him. What social life was there up here? Back home he always had a girl, though he avoided any serious entanglements. He couldn't afford that. Emotionally or financially.

"More coffee, anyone?" Marian asked, pouring for herself.

"None for me." Mel frowned. He hates me, Jason thought, hates me for being more than twenty years younger, ambitious, and confident. Mel vacillated between rage at the whole world, and periods of depression when he sat at meals without uttering a word. Frank had cautioned them to respect these periods, which appeared to be in retreat. But the inner rage remained.

"I'll have a cup, Marian," Herb decided belatedly.

Herb actually believed Marian was a towering success back in New York theater, Jason thought with mild contempt. Didn't he know she lived on unemployment insurance more than on her theater earnings? New York State unemployment insurance was subsidizing the arts.

Jason listened to the sound of Jill's voice as she talked to Clara out in the kitchen. Anticipating her approach, he rose and walked to the door.

"Jill?"

"Yes." She walked into view. Her face pink

78

from the cold. Looking beautiful. He was particularly susceptible up here, with nobody except
Frank's collection of misfits available for socializing. In New York he'd taken out girls more
spectacular than Jill.

"Come into the sitting room and have coffee.
Warm up before the fireplace."

"I've had my quota of coffee until after
dinner," she laughed. Her smile including the
others.

"What about a walk along the ocean?" Jason
pursued. "You haven't had a chance for that yet,
have you?"

"I'd love it," she accepted promptly. "But let
me thaw out my hands first." She was tugging at
her gloves. "Herb, how do you work with your
hands out there in that cold barn?"

"I don't notice," Herb said.

"How's the statue coming?"

"Oh, it's coming along fine." Herb's face
glowed. "It's the biggest thing you ever saw.
Back home I could never make anything more
than a foot high. I didn't have the room."

"I'll get my jacket," Jason said to Jill. "Be
down in five minutes."

Though Herb was almost twice Jason's age,
sometimes he looked at Herb and wondered
with sickening fear if he'd wind up in Herb's
shoes. No! Damn, he had more than a dilettante's ability. He had drive. He was impatient
because last month he'd hit thirty, and he
wanted to make it while he was young.

He'd stay here, finish the book, and go back to work — selling at Macy's or Alexander's — until the book sold and money started coming in. But not in Herb's shoes. He wouldn't let that happen.

Jill was waiting by the fire, her coat off, when Jason sauntered back into the sitting room. Was Frank romantically interested, Jason wondered. He had an odd way of looking at her for no reason at all. Jill was rich fare for a lonely man getting on. It could upset the applecart if Frank developed romantic ideas about Jill. He might not want the rest of them around.

"Ready to go?" What had brought Jill up here? She seemed too hardy to be knocked down by her first flop play. A love affair that backfired? "Is that coat warm?"

"Oh, yes." Jill smiled as she pulled on the coat. It was a double-breasted coachman's style with a woolen lining, "warm — and heavy."

They walked out of the cozy warmth of the house into the sharp outdoor chill. The mid-afternoon sun playing an in-and-out game.

"Wait a sec." Jason reached for Jill's arm. "Here comes Jed with the mail. Anything for me?" he called out. It was a habit to be expectant about the mail. Occasionally, in the past six years he'd sold a short story. But it was such a rotten market as magazines continued to fold. Besides, it wasn't his cup of tea. "Like a check for half a million?"

"The local newspaper," Jed drawled. "That's it for today."

"Be careful," Jason warned Jill as they cut around to the side of the house, to begin the sharp descent. "This path is rugged." Like the view below. And he anticipated Jill's gasp of appreciation as she caught her first sight, close up, of the turbulent Atlantic, the defiant rocky shore, the jagged cliff that dropped so terrifyingly to the coastline below.

"Oh, Jason, it's magnificent!"

They stood there at the top of the flagstone steps that led below. A precarious downward trip for the incautious. Both of them caught up in the rugged beauty before them. Then Jason's hand at her arm prodded her downward.

"How long does it take for mail to come up from New York?" Jill asked as they moved with care from step to step.

"Just a couple of days." Then there *was* a fellow down in New York.

"My father's in Peru. I wrote to him about my coming up here," Jill explained. "He'll probably think I'm out of my mind," she laughed. "Leaving New York and all. But I'm anxious to hear from him."

"It's the local mail that's sometimes slow. The newspaper's due out on Wednesday. We should have it on Thursday, but more times than not, it doesn't come until Friday." He chuckled. "Then Clara's in a dither because her mother

81

can't bear waiting that extra day for the local gossip."

"Clara's mother lives at Cliff House?" Jill asked in surprise.

"In the attic apartment, with Clara. You know that deck that shoots out on the roof?"

"Oh, yes." Jill recalled the part of the roof with the balcony.

"Frank built that for the old lady, I gather. She's eighty-three and presumably a semi-invalid. I suspect she's an old humbug. Don won't admit it, professional ethics," he drawled. "She's supposed to be hardly able to walk, but I surprised her late one night at the refrigerator downstairs. Making herself a ham and cheese sandwich. Guess they were out of it upstairs. Clara's bushed after a day's work — she wouldn't hear the old lady come downstairs."

"Poor Clara," Jill said with sympathy, and then paused to enjoy the view. The ocean churning into a furious white foam as it dashed against the rocks was only feet below now. "What a subject for an artist!"

"Mel walks here regularly, but he doesn't paint it. You'd think he would. I'll remember this," Jason went on humorously, "when I'm city-bound a year from now. I'll remember Maine, and all this turbulent nature."

"The city seems a million miles away, doesn't it?"

"I wouldn't want to stay here for a lifetime, but right now it's great."

"I could stay here forever," Jill said with quiet conviction, "if I could be involved in theater some way."

"In a village of two thousand?" Jason jeered. "When they talk about theater here, they mean the movie house. Of course, Maine's loaded with summer playhouses." But the winters could be long and grim.

"I didn't mean that," Jill said with unexpected passion. "I mean regional theater, on a year-round basis. You know how little distances mean up here. People think nothing of traveling twenty to thirty miles. Regional theater could take hold up here." Her eyes were mildly defiant. She expected cynicism from him. "I'll bet Frank could be a real force in establishing regional theater in Maine."

"Frank is busy right now being the published author." Jason looked down. Damn, he shouldn't have said that. He sounded like the others, with their injured egos.

"I'm dying to read Frank's book." Jill was gazing at him with a glint of reproach.

If she thought he was jealous of Frank's minor triumph she was wrong, Jason told himself. He had a rendezvous with the best-seller list. With staggering income tax problems. It wasn't enough for him to write, the way it was with some writers. He wanted all the fringe benefits, plus. The expensive cars and the Manhattan condominium high above Fifth Avenue. Winters in Jamaica, summers at St. Tropez. He wanted to make up for all the empty, lost, anguished years he spent in that rotten slum, with a father who didn't want him. Jason wanted the best of everything, to make up to the kid who'd cried himself to sleep until there were no more tears.

"You're asking for trouble, Jill," Jason said as he realized she was watching him with curiosity. "Let the book lie. Frank's had one disappointment that cut deep. Don't dig it up again."

"I was thinking he might be able to sell it for a paperback reprint." A faint hostility in her now? "My roommate in New York is an editor at a paperback house — I could get a reading for him. She told me that practically every novel they buy has a print run of close to a hundred thousand." Her eyes softened. "Wouldn't Frank adore knowing that a hundred thousand people read his book!"

"Look, he's built a life for himself." Jason's face tightened with rejection. "Don't expose him to fresh hurt. Suppose they turn him down? He doesn't need the money —"

"You don't have any faith in him, Jason!"

"Hi."

Jason tensed at the sound of Don Munson's voice. What was he doing here on the beach in the middle of the afternoon?

"Hi." A lilt of pleasure in Jill's voice. She liked Dr. Galahad. The realization annoyed Jason. "Taking a constitutional?" Jill asked.

"I'm parked right up there on the road." Don's smile included both Jill and Jason. "I decided on five minutes along the shore to clear my head. When I was a kid I used to spend my summers with my grandparents at the Rockaways." His eyes turned somber. "I hear the beach there has eroded so badly the tide comes almost up to the boardwalk these days."

"The summer people are trying like crazy to buy land up here, to build their shoddy cottages and spend their frantic ten weeks by the sea each year," Jason drawled. "But they're tough customers up here. They're hanging on to their land. Until the offering prices become irresistibly high," he guessed cynically.

"You settling in comfortably?" Don concentrated on Jill.

Was he going to make a pitch? Competition reared again in Jason. He might take a shot at her himself. More than a pretty face there. All right, a beautiful face, and figure to match. Jill Conrad was bright. It could be stimulating to spend a few weeks in pursuit of Jill. Nothing serious, he cautioned himself automatically. But in the hours away from the typewriter he could do some socializing with this girl and enjoy it. He hadn't expected this at Cliff House.

But this business about dragging out Frank's book could be a disaster for all of them. Frank, involved in writing again, would find houseguests a distraction. Jason needed these coming months at Cliff House to finish his book. He couldn't, at any cost, allow Frank to become interested in writing again!

"I'm having a great time," Jill said in response to Don's question. Jason noticed a sudden guarded quality in her eyes. "But people here in town look at me so strangely. As though I were a Martian!"

"They don't like Frank's guests. Don't worry about them." Jason rejected them with a scornful wave.

"It takes them a while to accept strangers," Don said. "It's taken them a while to accept me."

"I suppose we'll be seeing you tomorrow night?" Jason asked.

"Oh, sure. I never miss one of Frank's Saturday nights unless there's an emergency call." He glanced at his watch. "I've got to get cracking."

"What's Frank's Saturday night?" Jill asked when they resumed their stroll.

"On Saturday evenings Frank takes his guests to the local movie. Afterward there's a buffet supper at the house. That's the night Clara goes off to see her friend Hallie. And upstairs," he continued with dry humor, "Clara's mother sits in front of her TV set and tries to think of ways to make Clara's life miserable."

"Jason —" Jill hesitated. "What do you know about old Mrs. Webster?"

"Only what you know." But he was instantly attentive. "What's bothering you?"

"I walked by the house. I heard her talking with someone. She's terribly upset about my being here. I heard her say, 'Why did he bring that girl here? What is he trying to do?' "

"You don't know that she was talking about you," Jason countered.

"I do know," Jill insisted. "It fits right in with the pattern. I disturb people in this town. *Why, Jason?*"

Chapter Seven

Jill and Jason walked back toward the house, skirting the snow-blanketed gravesite, where nothing of the roses remained except the stems. The sun already in descent. The only sounds those of the waves hammering at the rocks below and, from inside the house, the erratic staccato of Mel's hunt-and-peck typing.

"In addition to the painting, Mel's writing a book," Jason reported dryly as they walked up the stairs to the porch. "He's writing it as a fictional journal. I gather his psychiatrist suggested it as a form of catharsis."

"He's so angry at the world. Just talking with him a few moments, you know he has this rage within him." She shivered faintly. People like Mel frightened her.

They cleaned their boots on the mat in front of the door, then Jason held the door wide for Jill, followed her inside.

"Go out to the kitchen and ask Clara to give you a mug of hot chocolate. You look half-frozen," Jason teased.

"I'm not," she protested. But she was chilled. The dampness of the sea. Marian's frightening sea.

"Go on. Clara enjoys feeling she's being put upon by Frank's guests. I'm going up to see if I can get some work done before dinner. I'd hit a snag. Maybe the fresh air cleared my head."

"Go work," she said with mock ferocity. She *was* enjoying being here — between bursts of apprehension. She hadn't thought once about the play closing since she'd arrived. She hadn't thought of Scott, who was in California now.

Jason headed up the stairs. From behind the double doors of the front sitting room Jill heard, as she walked down the corridor to the kitchen, the muted sounds of the TV. Marian would be watching.

"She's not the kind to be stayin' long," Clara was saying to someone in the kitchen. "You'll see." And then someone answered. A woman. Her voice so low the words didn't carry to Jill.

At Jill's approach over the uncarpeted segment of the corridor, the voices inside stopped. The speakers realized they'd be overheard.

Jill walked into the kitchen with a forced smile. "Jason and I just hiked along the beach." Clara's visitor was the younger woman from the cottage. Suddenly Jill's heart was pounding. "I was wondering if I could have some coffee to thaw me out." The percolator was always on the range.

"I'll get it for you." For a moment Clara's brooding eyes rested on Jill, then moved to the woman who sat at the table. "Thank you, Miss Kate, for lookin' in on Mama. She appreciates that."

Clara moved to the range. She had no intention of introducing the visitor, Jill realized. Clara couldn't wait to get the woman out of the kitchen.

"You know you can always call on me, Clara." The woman's eyes pointedly avoided Jill as she rose nervously.

"Don't forget the coffee cake for your aunt," Clara admonished, reaching for the foil-wrapped package that sat on the counter. "Glad she enjoyed the mince pie."

Jill intercepted the secretive exchange between the two women. What had they been talking about before she came in? *Something to do with her* "She's not the kind to be stayin' long." Clara meant her.

"Miss Kate's a registered nurse," Clara explained when they were alone. "Mrs. Webster's niece. She lives down in the cottage with her. Mama's eighty-three. I get nervous even when she has a cold, at her age and with her health bein' delicate." Clara was rambling on compulsively. "She's been delicate ever since I was born. I weighed just three pounds, and she was so worried about me she had a nervous breakdown. She never got back on her feet after that."

"It's nice that you have a nurse living so close." Jill made herself respond, but continued to wonder why her arrival upset old Mrs. Webster and why Clara and Kate were disturbed about her presence at Cliff House.

The rear door opened, bringing in a gust of

cold. Clara started at the unexpected sound. Herb came into the kitchen, blowing on his red, ungloved hands.

"This time of the afternoon the temperature sure drops." Herb's smile was friendly.

"I suppose you want some coffee, too," Clara asked sullenly.

"I wouldn't mind." Herb joined Jill at the table.

"I don't know how you stay out there in that barn with nothin' but that stove to keep you warm." Clara shook her head.

"I'm going to be through in two or three weeks," Herb said. "She's bigger than life, sitting out there astride her horse."

"What are you gonna do with it when you're finished?" Clara asked skeptically. "Leave it settin' out there in the barn?"

Herb's face fell. His eyes filled with reproach.

"I haven't much thought about that, Clara. I figure somebody in these parts might want to buy it. I'll have to talk to Frank about that," he said. "I can't take it home with me, that's for sure."

"You'll find a home for it," Jill said, touched by his insecurity.

Clara brought two cups of coffee to the table, returned to the sink to peel potatoes for dinner. The roast in the oven sent forth a savory aroma. The kitchen windows were pleasantly steamed over. An air of cozy serenity permeated the room.

Herb drank his coffee in eager gulps, relishing its warmth after the hours in the cold barn. He waited politely for Jill to finish hers. She sensed he was impatient to leave the room.

"Don't let me keep you, Herb," she said. "I'll sit here and sip forever."

"I just thought I'd see what Marian's watching on TV. It's relaxing, after I've been working out in the barn all day." He pushed back his chair and left.

"Ain't much to do here for a girl your age." Clara finally punctured the silence that fell between Jill and herself. "I told ya."

"Oh, I don't mind," Jill assured her. "I love being here." Except for these strange undercurrents that eroded her calm.

"You'll be tired of it soon enough. Don't say I didn't warn you," Clara said gloomily. "Nothin's more depressin' than Maine at the tail end of winter unless you got plenty to do to keep yourself occupied."

"I'll be all right," Jill said firmly. But she was relieved when Clara left the kitchen.

She sat alone at the table, sipping her coffee, her mind dissecting the odd occurrences at Cliff House. She didn't believe in Marian's messages from the sea, but at odd moments she recoiled from the hostility she felt in Marian. The others — Clara, Bill at the luncheonette, old Mrs. Webster — were alarmed by her presence here. But Marian resented her being at Cliff House. Marian *hated* her.

Jill slept late Saturday morning. When she awoke it was to a depressing display of sleet and snow outdoors. With a touch of guilt about her tardiness, she rose, dressed, went downstairs hurriedly.

Clara moved about the range watching a skillet of bacon, checking on the progress of biscuits in the oven.

"I don't know why everybody can't come down to breakfast at the same time, like civilized people," she grumbled. "Bacon oughta be served when it's just been drained."

Clara cracked eggs, dropped them into a frying pan, pulled the biscuits from the oven, drained the bacon. While Jill gazed distractedly outdoors, Clara slid eggs onto a plate, added strips of bacon, reached cautiously to dump a half-dozen tall, golden biscuits into a bowl, and transported both plate and bowl to the table.

"Mama says she'd like to meet you," Clara said self-consciously. "She used to be crazy about goin' to the theater, oh, twenty years ago when she was better able to get around. When you finish your breakfast, I'll take you upstairs to see her."

"Thank you, Clara, that'll be lovely." Was Clara's mother really a theater fan? Jill suspected not. Why was she anxious to meet Jill Conrad?

Marian sauntered in, nodded majestically to Clara, sat herself beside Jill. Always that covert hostility in her. But that wouldn't prevent

Marian from enjoying her breakfast. She adored being served here in the huge country kitchen, Jill thought. It was such a contrast to the decaying hotel in the West Seventies where Marian lived in New York. Though Marian tried to make a gay adventure of living in a tiny hotel room where a hot plate secreted in a closet served as a kitchenette.

A few minutes later, Herb arrived to join them. Herb was always flatteringly attentive to Marian, despite her occasional cutting remarks about his artistic talents. They settled down to discuss the evening movie, ignoring Jill.

"You ready to go up to see Mama?" Clara asked when Marian and Herb had been served. Jill was draining her second cup of coffee, her plate empty before her.

"Yes." Jill smiled and pushed back her chair. Aware of the astonished curiosity of the other two.

Together Jill and Clara climbed the stairs to the attic apartment. The living room was depressingly drab. The furniture an ill-assorted collection from the long years of the old lady's marriage. Clara's mother sat in an armchair placed at a window. Her salt-and-pepper hair cut girlishly short, highlighting its curliness, was incongruous above the deeply lined face. She stared absently at the sleet. Unaware of their approach.

"Mama," Clara said softly, and Mrs. Henderson swung about with a petulant frown.

"Clara, you startled me. I didn't hear the door open. I guess I was daydreamin'." Now her eyes settled intently on Jill. She leaned forward, the heavily veined hands gripping the arms of the chair. Searching every feature in Jill's face. *For what?* "So you're the new guest," she said with a sigh. "Frank'll be bringin' them up from the kindergarten next."

"Mama, I told Miss Conrad how you used to like to go to the theater," Clara said softly.

"Go get out them programs, Clara. Show them to her." Mrs. Henderson gestured impatiently.

"What a beautiful antimacassar!" Jill said, to fill in the heavy silence that suddenly fell between them.

"I used to sew beautifully as a girl." Mrs. Henderson preened remembering. "But of course, all that was over with Clara's birth. I never really recovered. But Clara takes after me with the sewing. Right after high school she went to work twice a week for the Websters, as a seamstress. People don't live like that no more. Nothin's like it used to be."

"Now Mama, don't start on that," Clara reproached.

But Mrs. Henderson, undaunted, began relating the saga of her ill health. Jill made a show of listening sympathetically. But beneath the too girlish tones, Jill detected something akin to hysteria.

At six-thirty sharp Frank good-humoredly

95

corralled his guests into the Bentley. Mel was sullen about being pushed into accompanying them.

"We'll make the seven o'clock performance," Frank promised. "We'll be back a few minutes past nine for that cold buffet supper Clara's going to leave for us. There'll be a few others coming, too." Frank obviously anticipated a festive evening.

"Clara's night to howl," Jason drawled, settling himself on the front seat beside Frank and Jill.

"Clara spends Saturday evenings with her friend Hallie. They grew up together," Frank explained. "Jed'll be at the house to make coffee and to take care of anything that requires heating before serving."

"What are we seeing tonight?" Marian asked, almost coquettishly, and the conversation turned to the movie being shown that evening.

At the tiny movie house Jason made a point of sitting beside Jill. Several times he whispered comments about the quality of the script in her ear. Frank, who sat on her other side, seemed irritated. Jill was relieved when the performance was over and they were leaving.

As the Bentley moved up the driveway at Cliff House, Jill spotted Don's car parked out front. He'd come early, perhaps, because he'd been on a case in the neighborhood. Don knew no such thing as a free day.

"Galahad's on time," Jason remarked. "He

can't resist Clara's cooking."

"That's not all that draws him to Cliff House," Marian said archly. She was in rare good humor today because Herb was being attentive. How nice for Marian and Herb, Jill thought, if that develops into something serious.

As they walked down the corridor toward the dining room, Don emerged from the library to meet them with a wide smile.

"I came early and chiseled coffee from Jed," he reported. "Visiting doctor claims special privileges."

The dining table, which normally seated eight, had been extended to accommodate an additional six. On the buffet sat platters of roast beef, baked ham, a whole turkey, a salad bowl. On a warming tray there was a casserole heaped high with golden mashed potatoes and another with home-frozen corn. At either end of the buffet sat an urn, one for coffee, one for Clara's locally famous hot punch. A portable bar had been set up, and Jason immediately appointed himself bartender. Don was sent to forage for ice cubes.

In a few minutes Phyllis Lattimer arrived. She was a small woman in her late fifties. Slender, hyperactive. Hair almost absurdly ringleted. Eyes large and heavily lashed, artfully made up, to a degree startling in a small Maine village. Once she must have been delicately beautiful, Jill decided.

Marian greeted her with astonishing cordiality. Phyllis Lattimer was the social arbiter of the town, with an avowed interest in the arts.

"This is Jill Conrad," Marian introduced her to Phyllis.

"Hello." Jill tried to be friendly. Difficult, because Phyllis glared at her with blatant dislike for one startling instant before she retreated behind a facade of pleasantness.

Jill was relieved when Chuck Travers, the expatriate from New York who ran the gift shop in town, sauntered into the dining room and headed for her.

Phyllis moved to the bar with Marian, where they waited to be served. Don returned with ice cubes, delivered them to Jason, hurried to join Jill and Chuck. Phyllis' eyes roamed about the room, following Frank. How long had Phyllis been trying to marry Frank, Jill wondered?

The doorbell rang. Jed hurried down the corridor to respond. Chuck Travers' gaze focused on the doorway. He was expecting someone. A smile touched his mouth as he heard the feminine voice at the door, discussing the weather with Jed.

Kate Meredith seemed faintly uneasy as she walked into the room. As though steeling herself to meet Frank's guests. Chuck crossed to the door to greet her. Her face lighted. She was pleased that he was here.

Frank allowed his guests to chat a while, then marshaled everybody to the buffet to serve themselves and settle about the extended dining room table. Phyllis and Marian contrived to flank

Frank. Chuck, at the other end of the table, was deep in conversation with Kate, who shot furtive stares in Jill's direction at odd moments.

"Clara's a great cook." Chuck turned to bring Don and Jill into his conversation with Kate. "She worked for your aunt years ago, didn't she, Kate?"

Kate colored faintly.

"I believe she did. That — that was before my time."

"We know you were a little girl then," Chuck smiled. "Were you old enough to remember Denise?"

Kate's eyes focused on her plate.

"I adored Denise. Everybody did."

"It makes it difficult for you," Don said sympathetically, "that Mrs. Webster maintains such total seclusion."

"Oh, I get out now and then," Kate answered. But nobody went into the house, Marian had told Jill. Except for Don and Hallie, who cleaned for Mrs. Webster two mornings a week. And Jed had said something about the fact that even he had never been invited in.

Just then Jed arrived to serve coffee or punch to the seated guests, taking his stand by the buffet with a look of martyrdom.

"Be adventurous and try Clara's hot punch," Frank prodded. "Clara's famous for it all over this county."

"I'll try it," Jill offered.

"Punch for me," Chuck added, and Don exuberantly raised his cup in agreement.

Jed solemnly served coffee first, then the cups of hot punch. Talking with Don and Chuck about regional theater, with which Chuck was familiar, Jill sipped the hot punch.

"Oh, it's great." She leaned back with a sense of well-being, smiled at Don, who sat beside her.

"I love this room," Chuck said with pleasure as he gazed about at the duplication of an old country manor dining room. "I think Frank's invitations to dinner regularly through the years is one of the reasons I stayed in town. I don't make a lot of money," he chuckled, "but there are these fringe benefits."

Jill frowned as a wild itching suddenly spread over her face. She reached compulsively to scratch. She was conscious, with a sense of panic, of a tightness in her throat, a difficulty in breathing. She tugged at the neckline of her dress. Gasping now for each breath. Don noticed, she realized. He was pushing back his chair, rising to his feet. His face was anxious.

"Don —" She fought to speak. "Don, I can't seem to breathe —"

She felt herself lapsing into unconsciousness. Struggling against it. Don was pulling her from her chair. Lifting her.

What was happening to her?

Chapter Eight

Don hovered anxiously over Jill. She was breathing all right now. Her color was better. Frank's having the oxygen in the house might have saved her life. Don had suggested the oxygen for Frank as a precaution in the event of another heart attack.

"She's all right," Don said encouragingly to Frank, who was white with alarm. Kate was wheeling away the oxygen with an air of relief. "It was only a bad allergic reaction."

"Allergic reactions can be frightening," Kate said gently to Frank as she returned to stand beside the bed.

"What was it?" Frank asked.

"Probably cinnamon," Don explained. As soon as he'd seen her gasping like that, noticed the itchiness, he'd remembered the first day he'd met her. She'd turned down the apple pie because of an allergy to cinnamon.

"There's no cinnamon in the punch!" Clara frowned at Don from the doorway. "I been makin' it for close to twenty years. Nutmeg but never a drop of cinnamon."

"Maybe Jill's allergic to something else," Frank suggested, then moved forward anxiously because Jill's eyelids were flickering uncertainly.

"Wow!" she whispered huskily, eyes wide, and smiled up at Don. "I didn't realize until I was going out that there was cinnamon in the punch."

"Not a drop of cinnamon goes into that recipe," Clara repeated firmly. "I can show it to you."

"Clara, there must have been," Jill protested.

"Wasn't no cinnamon in it when I poured it into the urn." Clara was upset. "Who coulda done it?"

"Some compulsive recipe meddler," Frank guessed. "You know how some people like to change things around."

"Clara, bring me a cup of punch, please," Don requested casually. "Let's make sure there is cinnamon in it before we name the allergy."

"I'll get it." Clara moved down the corridor.

"That's my allergy," Jill said stubbornly. "I've been through the whole test routine."

"Anybody could have added the cinnamon," Don acknowledged. Anybody with access to the dining room. Was it a meddling mistake, or something less innocuous? "Somebody might just have been intent on spicing up the punch behind Clara's back," Don continued with studied matter-of-factness, "without being aware of Jill's allergy." But all the guests at Cliff House had been in the library when Jill said she was allergic to cinnamon. Don was busy with a needle now; reached for Jill's arm. "This is going to put you to sleep for the night," he teased. "Don't expect to do any more socializing this evening."

"I've had quite enough." She laughed shakily.

He'd been scared to death for a couple of minutes. How had she become so special in such a short time? It was rough to keep his head around Jill Conrad.

Frank and Don waited until Jill dropped off, just as Clara arrived, panting from this second climb up the stairs in a short while, with a mug of the punch. Silently she extended the mug to Don. He took it, sniffed, concentrated, tasted.

"Cinnamon," he confirmed.

"I thought so, too," Clara said heavily. "Who'd have the nerve to go messing with my punch that way?" she demanded indignantly.

"Fortunately Don was here." Frank tried to sound undisturbed. "Should Clara sit here with Jill for a while?"

"That isn't necessary. A good night's sleep, and she'll be back to normal. Just scared her for a few minutes," Don said. Why couldn't he accept the logical theory that somebody tampered with the punch without knowing of Jill's allergy? "Come on," he said briskly. "Let's all go downstairs again."

The others were sitting around the library, talking in the quiet tones motivated by Jill's sudden, unexpected collapse. Jason leaned forward with a questioning look of concern.

103

"Is she all right?" Chuck's eyes moved from Don to Kate.

"A bad allergic reaction. She's fine now." Don checked his watch. "I'd better be getting home. Hospital rounds at seven in the morning." Actually, he wanted to stop by the hospital for a few minutes tonight. He'd sleep better if he checked out the Miller boy, who'd been brought in for an emergency appendectomy. Dr. McTavish was on evening duty, but he was apt to be in a rush.

"I'd better be going, too." Kate rose nervously.

"I'll take you down the driveway." Chuck was on his feet, solicitous for Kate.

Don wondered why Chuck couldn't get anywhere with Kate. He'd been trying for years, Frank said — ever since she returned from England. God knows, Kate seemed to want something more than this casual relationship. Was she waiting for the old lady to die?

Frank walked with them to the door. Outside, in the damp cold of the night, with the moon in hiding behind clumps of dark clouds, Don lingered briefly with Chuck and Kate before getting into his own car.

"Clara seemed particularly upset," Chuck said thoughtfully. "About Jill's attack, I mean. I suppose because she was here in the house when Denise fell from that window."

"What does that have to do with Jill?" Kate's voice was unexpectedly belligerent.

"Nothing," Chuck soothed, taking her arm. "Except, somehow, you don't expect lightning to strike twice."

"It didn't," Kate pointed out. "Jill's all right." But Kate Meredith was deeply agitated.

Don slid behind the wheel of his car, moved down the driveway ahead of Chuck. His eyes searched the sky as he moved out onto the road. He hoped they weren't in for snow again.

He leaned forward to flip on the radio, fiddled with the dial with one hand until he found a music program. Thinking about Jill, he headed for the hospital.

The hospital wore its muted night appearance as he drove into the parking area. Most of the rooms were dark. A stillness pervaded the reception room as he walked briskly inside. The nurse at the desk, checking charts, greeted him with a smile.

"I'll take a look at the Miller kid," Don said, striding toward the stairs. "Everything on an even keel around here?"

"No problems. McTavish is floating around somewhere on two," the nurse reported. "He brought a patient in."

Don headed directly for the Miller child's room. Approaching the doorway he saw Maggie Ryan's massive figure bent over the bed. The compassionate, stubborn-jawed head nurse — forty years a nurse with the hospital, twenty-two of them in her present capacity — brushed a strand of hair from the small boy's face.

"Good-evening, Maggie," he said softly.

Maggie turned around.

"A worrier, Doctor?" Maggie drawled. But Maggie Ryan, also, was a worrier.

"Nothing else to do with my time," he shot back with a grin.

"What are you doing here?" Dr. McTavish's gruff voice interrupted from the corridor.

"Just stopped by for a few moments." Don refused to be ruffled.

"You up at Danzig's place tonight?" McTavish's eyes were probing. "Noticed you left that number at the desk for calls."

"I dropped by for a while." What the devil business was it of McTavish's where he went on Saturday evenings?

"He still got that girl there?"

"She's just arrived." Signals were jogging up in Don's mind. What did it mean to McTavish that Jill was staying at Cliff House? Was he just a nosy old man?

"He going senile or something?" McTavish's voice was laced with disgust. Or was it anger? "Why did he bring her up here?"

"Why not? He's always bringing up guests from the city." Don's eyes concentrated on McTavish.

"Why this particular girl?" McTavish demanded in a burst of irritation. "What's he trying to stir up?"

"What do you mean, Dr. McTavish?" Don pretended mild curiosity, but bells were clanging in his head. *What was McTavish afraid that Jill's presence would stir up?*

McTavish glared at him, his eyes dark, mouth tight. Realizing he'd spoken more freely than he'd intended.

"A man his age having a girl like her in his house?" McTavish was trying to bluff his way out. "People are going to talk — you ought to know that."

"About Frank?" Don scoffed. "With all those guests in his house?"

McTavish grunted, ambled off without further conversation. Maggie was engrossed in checking the Miller boy's chart.

It was specifically Jill who upset McTavish. And earlier this evening somebody was sufficiently upset by her presence to put cinnamon in that punch. What was going on?

As Don moved down the corridor to look in on another patient, he could hear McTavish's vintage Chevy move into action. No use trying to pump the old man. He wasn't going to talk. But there were a lot of questions building up in Don's mind — and he was going to start looking for answers.

Chapter Nine

Jill stirred beneath the blankets, vaguely conscious that it was late in the morning. Both Jason and Mel typed somewhere in the house, in furious disharmony. The sun filtered through the drapes, high in the sky, strong for this time of year.

Slowly the night before came back to her vividly. And she was jarred into full wakefulness. She'd slept heavily because of the injection. Except for a mild headache, no aftereffects from the allergy attack.

Someone had deliberately spiked the punch, knowing it would be disastrous for her. No, she couldn't accept Frank's suggestion that someone had tampered with the recipe.

Now she was restless. Impatient to be dressed and out of her room. Out of bed and in a robe, she crossed to a window that faced the Atlantic. The sky a delicate, hint-of-spring blue. The sunlight dazzling. A strong wind whipped the winter-bare boughs of the trees into frenzy. Below, the waves thrust violently against the rocky shoreline.

Despite a nagging unease, she felt an insistent hunger. Go on downstairs, out to the kitchen for coffee. Quickly she dressed and left the room.

A phone rang below as she started down the stairs.

"Jed, you call upstairs and tell Miss Conrad there's a phone call for her. Yell loud, she'll hear," Clara ordered.

Jill leaned over the banister.

"I'm on my way down —"

Jed hovered before a wall sconce, changing a light bulb.

"You can take it in the library," he said, without looking at her. Absorbed in his small task.

"Thank you."

Jill skimmed past him, turned into the library, crossed directly to the desk to pick up the phone.

"Hello —"

"How're you feeling?" Don's voice. Solicitous, reassuring — and beautifully welcome.

"I feel fine. Thanks to you."

"Take it easy today," he ordered. "I'll buzz you tonight. I've got a rough day ahead, a couple of minor emergencies. I doubt that I'll be able to drop by."

"Thanks for everything," she said softly.

He had a rough day, but he'd bothered to take out these few minutes to check on her. Don Munson was a special person.

Jill went out into the kitchen, deserted at the moment. Coffee simmered on the range. She took down a mug from the row that hung beneath a cabinet, filled it, walked with it to the table. How good it felt here in the comfortable warmth of the kitchen, with the sun spilling through the windows.

"You feelin' all right this mornin'?" Clara came into the kitchen with a look of anxiety on her face.

"I'm fine," Jill reassured her. "And ready for breakfast."

"A nice omelet?" The brooding in Clara's eyes replaced by solicitude this morning. "I'll put some bacon and cheese in it. That makes it mighty tasty."

"Sounds great," Jill said. Don't think about last night. Just about this moment. *Relax.*

"Mr. Danzig asked if I'd seen you when he left with Mr. Bronson for church this morning. I told him I expected you were still sleepin'. And you'd wake up right as rain."

Marian walked in. Eyes brightly inquiring. Hostility apparently wiped out by last night's mishap.

"How're you feeling?"

"Fine." Jill returned her smile.

"You frightened us all." Marian crossed to seat herself at the table. "But I wasn't entirely surprised. Remember the day you arrived?" Marian's voice acquired the odd quality that, to Jill, was like chalk dragged across a blackboard. "I told you something dreadful would happen to you. The sea said this to me!" She leaned forward, her eyes compelled Jill to be attentive. "You'll find more trouble if you stay. Go back to

New York. Go back where you'll be safe."

Clara had turned away from the range. As she stared at them, her nearsighted eyes seemed fearful.

"Last night was just an absurd accident." Jill tried to sound calm. Why couldn't Marian drop the melodrama. Marian simply wanted her to leave Cliff House. She resented Frank's interest in *her*. "Nothing else is going to happen to me."

Don't think about last night. Don't think about the strangeness that hit at her from every side in this town. She couldn't leave now. Not with this feeling building in her that these weeks at Cliff House were to change the course of her life.

After breakfast Jill returned to her room, ostensibly to write letters. She felt uncomfortable downstairs with Marian. Jason still typed in his room. Mel had abandoned his own efforts at the typewriter. She could hear him pacing inside as she passed his room on the way to her own.

Jill stretched across the bed to read, but her mind refused to focus on the words, returning, instead, to last night's near-disaster. If Don hadn't been there, she might have died.

She laid aside the book, crossed to the desk to sit down and write to Sheila. But, again, she found it difficult to concentrate. All at once she was impatient to be out of the house. To breathe fresh outdoor air.

She went to the closet, pulled down her parka,

checked to be sure gloves were in the pocket, and darted from the room. Glad that she encountered no one on her way to the front door.

The sky was gray. A threat of snow hovered in the air. Jill followed the cleaned-off path to the right of the house. Pulling the parka snugly over her head, she buttoned it tight about her throat. She reached for her gloves, walking without direction.

She moved quickly. Impatient to put the house behind her. The barn loomed tall and austere against the winter sky, but something was wrong —

She gazed with sudden unease at the flare of light from the barn. Herb was in church. Could there be a fire? Her eyes settled on the door, left ajar. Go over and have a look.

She strode quickly, anxious to reach the door, to gaze within. Before she was quite there, she heard a voice inside and stopped in her tracks. Mel Citron's voice.

"He calls that a piece of sculpture?" Mel was saying in contempt. "My kids could do better." She moved to the door, curious to see with whom he was speaking. His back was to her. A kerosene lamp in his hand as he stood before the huge, awkward piece of sculpture. Alone. "Oh, God!" Suddenly his voice was anguished. "What am I doing up here? What am I doing to my family? What's happening to me that I do these awful things? What's happening?"

Guilty at her intrusion into this private

moment, Jill swung about, hurriedly retraced her steps. But Mel's words echoed in her brain. Had Mel put cinnamon in the punch, was that one of the "awful things"?

Inside the house again, Jill went directly up the stairs to her room. Marian was at her familiar stand before the TV set in the small sitting room, oblivious of her. As Jill walked into her room, she heard a car pulling up the driveway. That would be Frank and Herb returning from church.

For a few minutes she busied herself, re-arranging her dresser drawers. Later she'd go for a long walk along the beach, Jill promised herself. She loved the sea. She'd walk after the heavy Sunday dinner, which Clara promised to serve around two. She felt a certain excitement knowing that Don would call in the evening — not a doctor calling a patient, she was sure. She would be in the house for that call.

The sun, which had been so brilliant a half-hour ago, had disappeared behind gray clouds. Jill switched on a lamp to relieve the dreariness. She walked to a window, gazed out at the gaunt winter landscape.

This would have been a perfect day to settle down with Frank's book, she decided. She must coax him to dig out a copy for her to read. And then suddenly she started at a loud report — a gun being fired — at the same instant the piercing of the window glass, the whizzing near her ear.

For a bewildered second she was immobile. Staring at the hole in the window just to the right of her head. *Someone had shot at her.*

Get back! Away from the windows! Her heart pounding, she made her way toward the door, hugging the walls. Another gunshot. And then a third and a fourth. None apparently hitting the window this time. This was unreal! It couldn't be happening!

She hurried from the room. Down the stairs. Her breathing labored. Marian and Herb sat together before the TV, engrossed in the program. Neither had heard the shots. She hurried down the corridor, searching for Frank.

Frank was in the library reading the Sunday papers. Jed was just putting a cup of coffee before him.

"Frank, I —" she said as he looked up with a smile.

"How're you feeling, Jill?"

"I was feeling fine until a minute ago." She took a deep breath, searching for words. Aware of her anxiety. "Somebody fired a gun at me. I was standing at a window in my room, just looking out — and suddenly there was this barrage of shots. One of them hit the window."

Instantly Frank was on his feet. Jed gaped in astonishment.

"I thought I heard poachers again," Jed said. "Even on Sunday. But to hit a window of the house!" He shook his head in disgust.

"Jed, you call the police chief and tell him we've got poachers again. I won't have it! Tell him somebody hit a window. Jill might have been killed." His eyes were distraught as they settled on her. "Let's go take a look at that window."

"Has this happened before?" Jill asked Frank shakily as they mounted the stairs.

"We're constantly finding hunters shooting on the property," Frank admitted. "But they've never come this close to the house. I've seen them emerge from the edge of the woods and chase after small game. Despite all of the 'No Trespassing' signs about the grounds. But this is too much."

In her room, still wary because her fear was so fresh, Jill walked to the window where she'd been standing minutes ago, pointed to the hole.

"The bullet's somewhere in the room." Frank's eyes scanned the walls. "If we can find it, we'll give it to the chief. Though I doubt he'll be able to track down the gun. Too many people in these parts hunt. Legally or illegally."

A moment later Frank froze before a segment of wall. He leaned forward intently.

"It's in here," he said. "Imbedded in the plaster. I'll have to send Jed up to dig it out. He'll take it down to the chief, see what he can find out about the owner. Though I don't expect much success," Frank gazed unhappily at Jill. "What a terrible time we're giving you here. I hope you won't let this drive you away?"

"Absolutely not." Jill's smile was determined. But she didn't believe she had been the near-victim of a hunter's wild shots.

She had been the hunted.

Chapter Ten

Mrs. Sommers ushered the last patient out of the office, reached for her coat and car keys, waved good-night to her boss, and left. Don yawned, crossed to stretch out on his Danish modern sofa for a few minutes. He'd been on the go for close to eleven hours, he estimated.

Last night there had been a 2 a.m. call that carried him all the way to the other side of town on a false alarm. But he always told his patients to phone if something appeared serious, no matter what the time. It had been indigestion instead of a heart attack. But the patient had a history of two previous heart attacks and a conscientious doctor didn't gamble.

It was the call to Jill that disturbed him. How could Frank be so sure that a poacher was responsible for that bullet hole in Jill's bedroom window? After that business with the cinnamon in the punch!

The first sight of Jill had made him realize the void in his life. Up until that moment he'd been sure he had everything he needed.

She'd come up here, running from something. Like all of Frank's guests. Could she settle for living for the rest of her life in a town like this?

He frowned. What the devil was the matter with him? He'd just met Jill Conrad. How did he know what went on inside her mind? Too little socializing. He was overly susceptible.

He reached to turn off the lamp at the end table, allotting himself a half-hour nap before he drove over to Bill's for the pork chop special. He was asleep almost immediately. Twenty minutes later, the sound of his doorbell intruded.

At first he ignored the ringing, shifting into a position on his side. Reluctant to relinquish sleep. And then, from habit, his mind responded to the summons.

"Just a minute." He swung his feet to the floor, yawned tiredly, geared himself for a last-minute invasion. Everybody in town was beginning to realize he was accessible on the old-fashioned basis. McTavish told him he was an ass.

He pulled the door wide, gazed with quick concern when he saw Frank Danzig standing there.

"I figured I'd drop by and coax you out to the house for dinner," Frank said. "You game?"

"I'm always game," Don answered good-humoredly. "You know that." For a moment he'd been afraid Frank might be in trouble. That was because Clara was always scared he might have another heart attack.

"Come out with me. Jed'll drive you home. I don't like the looks of your snow tires."

"It's late in the year to buy new ones," Don said apologetically.

"These were old when you got them," Frank reminded him. "We've got some spares in the garage that are the same size as yours — and in a lot better condition. I'll tell Jed to bring them in when he drives you home. Can't have you laid up from an accident," he chuckled.

"Thanks." Don was casual in his gratitude. Frank would be embarrassed by any real demonstration. "Let me get my coat."

He sensed that Frank was in the mood for talk. That little twitch in his left eyelid gave away his tension. All week Frank had been tense.

"What do you think of Jill Conrad?" Frank asked when they were seated in the Bentley. "Pretty."

"She's lovely." Frank wasn't going to become emotionally involved with Jill, Don wondered. She was about a third his age! In the dark of the car he shot an anxious glance at Frank.

"I figured she'd be some diversion for you," Frank said slyly. "Not that I wouldn't have invited her up without an ulterior motive." The Bentley moved out of the driveway onto the road.

"Frank, Jill isn't going to be interested in a country doctor," Don protested. He was sure Frank hadn't brought Jill to Cliff House because the local doctor might be suffering from a lack of social contact. Most of the time Frank seemed disarmingly open, but there was something hidden in the cavern of his mind that he wasn't revealing now. Could it be that Frank meant to use him as a cover for his own romantic interest in Jill? The conjecture was disturbing.

Frank had been near death, Don reminded himself. After the heart attack he'd opened his house to strangers because he wanted to make up for the empty years behind him. He enjoyed the companionship of people from the city. People with creative leanings.

Last night Frank's eyes had moved to Jill, wherever she stood in the room. But Frank was too bright, too realistic, to believe there could be a future for Jill and himself.

The house seemed richly inviting as Frank opened the door for Don. The lighting of the foyer displayed Frank's fine furniture with a museum-like mellowness. The cozy warmth of the lower floor, enhanced by the aroma of dinner on the kitchen range, wrapped him in comfort. From the library record player came the score from *Fiddler on the Roof.*

Jed, pulling on a car coat, came with awkward haste toward them. He must have heard the car drive up.

"I'll put away the Bentley, Mr. Danzig. And Clara says to wash up and go right into the dining room. Dinner's ready to be served."

Jed's face was unexpectedly wary as he glanced toward someone coming down the stairs. Not wary, Don corrected himself. Alarmed.

Jill was coming down the stairs wearing a sunlight yellow pantsuit that made her seem taller, more sophisticated. There was a strained air about her that tied in with the look of alarm Jed had shot in her direction. Instinctively Don swung his eyes from Jill to Frank. If Frank suspected anything wrong, he was not revealing it.

"Hi." Jill's voice was warm.

"Hi." Don's eyes rested appreciatively on her.

"I'm going to wash up." Frank was headed for the downstairs bathroom, deliberately leaving him alone with Jill. "Clara's champing to put dinner on the table."

"You look lovely," Don said.

"Thank you." Her smile grew more relaxed.

"Frank came by and dragged me along for dinner. Of course," he chuckled, "all he has to do is whistle and I run. Bill's dinner menu is awfully predictable."

"Aren't the smells from the kitchen tantalizing?" She sniffed with an exaggerated twitch of her nose, and suddenly he could imagine her onstage.

No, don't think of her as an actress. Actresses are inaccessible city people. What the devil's the matter with me? Reacting like a fourteen-year-old with a first romance!

He forced himself into impersonal conversation as they strolled toward the dining room. "Did you know that Cliff House dates back to the early 1800s? I understand it was a station on the Underground Railroad." He liked the way she moved. The way she walked — leaning forward slightly, as though eager to meet the world head-on. "Frank's quite proud of that."

"Don, what about the girl who's buried out front? What do you know about her?"

"Only that she was talking to someone on the beach below — and she leaned too far from the window and fell to her death. She went to school with Frank and Clara."

"Did Clara go to school with Frank?" Jill found this intriguing. "And now she calls him Mr. Danzig?"

"Dr. Galahad —" Jason grinned at them from the doorway. "Staying for dinner, I presume?" A sardonic amusement in his eyes.

"Frank insisted." Don tried not to let Jason ruffle him. Jason had a talent for that.

Marian was already at the dining table, as were Herb and Mel. As usual, Marian was holding court. She resents Jill's being here, Jill has stolen her thunder, Don realized. She looks at Jill and sees herself forty years ago. And there is no going back.

Frank, the last to arrive, apologized for delaying dinner. The moment he was seated, Jed began to serve. Jason was turning on the charm full-blast — to impress Jill — and Don was annoyed. How long was Jason going to hang around milking Frank?

Over Clara's excellent leg of lamb Jill diverted the conversation from Marian's apparently completed account of a road tour six years earlier. Jill hadn't meant to be rude but Marian seethed.

"Frank, have you dug up a copy of your

book?" Jill leaned forward eagerly.

Frank's book? Don turned to him with astonishment.

"I opened my big mouth a few nights ago," Frank said with a deprecating smile. "It was the thirtieth anniversary of the publication of my one novel."

"You wrote a novel, Frank?" Don was genuinely impressed.

"You see?" Frank joked. "Not even my doctor believes me."

"You promised to let me read it," Jill reminded him.

"I will. I've got some copies stuck away in the storeroom out in the barn. I'll get one out for you over the weekend." Frank smiled at Clara, who came into the room with another bowl of mashed potatoes.

Nobody else at the table seemed keen on reading Frank's book. Were they nervous about having to make a favorable comment when they suspected the book would be awful? But it had been published, Don considered. Somebody thought it was good.

"I'd like to read it, too." Don spoke on impulse. Filling a lull in the conversation. "May I?"

"Of course." Frank's eyes lighted. He was enjoying, with some inner trepidation, this minor interest in his literary labor. "Oh, Marian —" Frank turned to her with a bright smile. "I forgot to tell you I spoke with Phyllis. She's interested in having you do a reading for her Ladies Club meeting. She'll be calling you."

"Oh?" Marian pretended to consider the proposal, but she was obviously delighted. "I suppose I could bring together some material that they would enjoy."

"Talk to Phyllis about it," Frank urged. "I'm sure you can work out a beautiful program for them. We don't have much theater up here, you know."

"I could do a reading from some of Shaw's heroines," Marian decided. A glint of anticipation in her eyes. "There are some marvelous passages. You have Shaw in your library, don't you, Frank?"

"The whole works," Frank conceded, and sat back to allow Marian full stage.

Marian was still holding forth on theater when Jed appeared in the doorway.

"You want dessert and coffee in here or in the library, Mr. Danzig?" Frank always had dessert and coffee, served in the library when there were guests, Don recalled; but Jed religiously made this inquiry.

"In the library, Jed," Frank instructed him.

As they left the dining room to cross to the library, Don made a conscious effort to engage Jill's attention. Jason was talking to Frank about his novel — to needle the others, Don decided with distaste.

"Do you ice-skate?" he asked Jill, moving her toward a pair of chairs in a far corner of the room while the others congregated around the fireplace.

"I try," she laughed. "I brought my skates along."

"If I can swing a free afternoon later in the week, would you like to run over to the lake to skate with me? I'll even bring along a thermos of hot chocolate." He enjoyed her lively interest in everything. She had been genuinely eager to read Frank's book. Nothing phony about Jill Conrad. She might act impulsively and afterward regret it — but she was beautifully honest.

"I'd love to go skating with you," Jill said. "When?"

"I'll buzz you tomorrow evening or Wednesday morning. By then I'll know how the week is shaping up."

At ten he rose reluctantly to say good-night. He had promised to run upstairs to have a look at Clara's mother before he left. Clara appreciated that. The old lady sat up watching TV until all hours. It wasn't too late.

"Remember, we're skating one afternoon this week," he said quietly to Jill before he left the gathering in the library.

"I'm looking forward to it."

Climbing up the second flight that led to the attic floor, he heard the faint hum of the television in the old lady's living room. He knocked lightly.

"Come in." She wasn't surprised. He often made these late little visits.

Mrs. Henderson was settled in her favorite armchair, before the television set. A blanket tucked about her for extra warmth.

"You're up late," he scolded, grinning. It was a running routine with them.

"At my age I can afford it," she shot back. When he'd first examined her, she'd cut seven years off her age. Clara had told him the truth. She was vain about her age and her thinness, which people took for delicacy. A thinness, he had to admit, that had helped her survive into her eighties. "Clara told me you were coming for dinner. She's sleeping already." Mrs. Henderson frowned with annoyance. She would have liked Clara to sit with her until past midnight.

He checked her pulse with the note of seriousness she enjoyed. She could last another ten years — or she could go tomorrow.

"You see that girl Frank brought here?" she asked abruptly.

"Yes." Signals shot up in his mind.

"You think she's pretty?" Her eyes focused sharply on him.

"Very." But it wasn't Jill's prettiness that brought that odd anxiety into her old eyes.

"How long's she stayin'?"

"I don't know." Why was she concerned?

"He shouldn'ta brought her here." Her voice was flat, grim.

"Why?" He watched her closely.

"That girl don't belong in this town." Her mouth pursed up. Her eyes studied the opposite wall. She wasn't going to open up.

"Why not?" he demanded.

"You like her, tell her to go back to the city where she comes from. Go back before she's sorry!" Then she raised the volume of the TV — she had lowered it on Don's entrance — signaling the fact that she had said all she was going to say about Jill's presence at Cliff House.

All the way home Don mentally ran a replay of his brief exchange with Mrs. Henderson. She was an old lady, he told himself. Probably alone more than she should be. Clara complained about yet another guest at Cliff House — and she was trying, deviously, to lighten Clara's load. Yet unease nagged at him, he was sure there was more to it than that.

Chapter Eleven

In pajamas and robe Jill settled on the edge of a chair before the russet glow in the fireplace. Nightly Jed started a fire in all the bedroom fireplaces because the heating on the upper floors, despite all Frank's efforts to have the furnace upgraded, couldn't quite cope.

She could hear the faint hum of voices downstairs. The others were talking late in the library. But once she'd begun to yawn, Frank had banished her upstairs.

Now ready for bed she was wide awake. Her mind assaulted by a barrage of questions for which she could find no answers. Don was deeply attracted to her. She'd have to be blind not to notice. She liked Don. She felt so comfortable with him. So relaxed. There was a gentleness about him that was most appealing.

But Jason was a challenge. He made her feel defensive. There was a lot of Scott in Jason. She'd been terribly hurt, so quickly, by Scott. She wouldn't let that happen again.

Restless, she left the fireplace, crossed to the window that looked out upon the sea. Fog was rolling in — massive whiteness — cutting the house off from the rest of the world. Jill shivered.

Not from the cold.

She left the window that looked down upon the sea to cross to one facing the front. The fog lay less heavy there, but still lent an eerie atmosphere as it settled down about the fenced-in plot where Denise Webster's body lay. Why did everybody say just so much about Denise's death, and then refuse to say more?

Suddenly she tensed. Her eyes strained to pierce the opaque blanket that threatened to make the house an island. What was that light in the area of the barn? An odd light. No, it wasn't a light. A fire! The barn was on fire!

She quickly surged into action. Darting to the door, she swung it wide and ran into the corridor. The voices were a low hum in the library below.

"Frank!" she called out, hurrying down the stairs. "Frank!" They were miles from a firehouse. Every moment counted.

"What is it?" Frank was hurrying down the lower floor corridor. "Jill, are you all right?"

Her voice was breathless from exertion as she leaned over the banister. Jason was trailing Frank now, his face etched with alarm. "There's a fire in the barn."

"Marian, phone the fire department," Jason called briskly before Frank could speak. "Dial the operator."

"There are hoses in the toolshed near the barn," Frank said, moving toward the corridor closet for a coat. "There's a faucet there. We've got fair pressure." He reached inside the closet, pulled out a coat for himself, another to toss to Jason. "Mel, wake Jed," he ordered as Mel appeared. "He sleeps in that room off the kitchen. Tell him to give you one of the extinguishers we keep around the house and bring out another himself. All right, Jason, let's go!"

Jill raced upstairs, trembling now, to change. With dramatic swiftness she got into slacks and parka, dug out her boots. The eerie siren that was the call to the local volunteer firemen screamed out through the night. When Jill came downstairs, Marian stood on the porch, shivering without a coat, watching the blaze that was visible through the thick fog.

"Marian, go inside before you catch cold," Jill ordered. She glanced upward. Clara was probably asleep. Her mother watching television. The old lady wouldn't notice the fire.

"Frank shouldn't be out there with his heart condition," Marian objected. "Why didn't you go quietly to Jed and tell him?"

"I didn't think," Jill stammered. Marian was furious with her. She was constantly making Marian furious.

"The fire can't reach the house, can it?" Fear clouded Marian's voice.

"They'll get the fire under control," Jill soothed. Frank said there was fair pressure. Was that enough?

It seemed incongruous for the barn to be

burning when the ocean was only two hundred feet away. How had the fire started? That kerosene lamp Mel had out there. Had he carelessly left it behind? "Put on some coffee, Marian," she urged gently. "I'll see if there's anything I can do out there. Maybe I can take them coffee when it's ready."

"I'll put it on." Marian was unexpectedly meek.

Jill hurried down the porch stairs, cut through the side path toward the barn. The snow had watered down to slush. The blaze was concentrated in one corner of the barn. Frank held a hose on the flames. Mel and Jason were using the extinguishers to try to keep the flames from moving further into the barn. Jed was unwinding a second, recalcitrant length of hose.

"Good thing Herb's sleeping," Mel said, faintly breathless with exertion. "He'd flip his lid if he thought something was going to happen to that chunk of stone inside."

"What's taking the fire department so long?" Jill felt futile as an onlooker.

"They're all volunteers," Frank reminded. "They've got to get dressed and over to the fire house."

As Frank talked, they heard the shrill siren of the fire truck, and moments later saw it turn in at the driveway below. A light was turned on in the cottage. Mrs. Webster and Kate had heard the siren.

The shining new truck pulled to a stop. Half a

dozen men leaped down, moved into action. Despite the seriousness of the situation, there was an air of adventure about them, Jill thought. These volunteer firemen enjoyed pitting themselves against the elements.

A fireman took the hose from Frank, moved in with exuberant determination. Then suddenly he yelled in alarm.

"Hey, Mr. Danzig, get outta there!"

Frank was moving into the open door of the barn. In the light of the fire Jill saw the stark intensity of his face. The storeroom, she thought. He's going to try to get his books out of the storeroom.

"Mr. Danzig, get out!" A fireman darted after him. "That roof could collapse!"

Jill moved forward anxiously. Another fireman firmly urged her back beyond the danger line.

"Mr. Danzig's in there!" Her eyes were wide with alarm. "Frank, come out!"

"Joe'll bring him out," the fireman assured her. "See, here they come now."

Frank was white with frustration. Holding his right hand slightly ahead of him.

"You'd better get up to the house and take care of that hand," Joe said gently. "We'll get this under control in a few minutes."

"Come up to the house and let me pack your hand in ice," Jill prodded. "We'll call Don."

"No need to bother Don," Frank demurred. But he winced in pain.

Marian paled when she saw them come into

the kitchen. "What happened?"

"Nothing serious." Frank tried to control his voice. "I got overzealous, tried to get some things out of the storeroom in the barn."

"I'll bring out the ice cubes." Jill was moving to the refrigerator.

"For a burn?" Marian was indignant. "Vaseline. I know Clara keeps a jar here in the kitchen." Her eyes moved frantically about the room.

"We'll pack his hand in ice cubes." Jill was already dumping out the tray. "Call Don. Tell him what happened."

Marian wavered, then crossed to the kitchen extension to call.

"Is the fire bad?" Clara, in a plaid flannel robe over her long nightgown, hovered in the doorway. "Mama heard the sirens. She woke me up. She's awful nervous. Should I try to bring her downstairs?"

"Let her stay," Frank ordered. "They'll have the fire under control in no time."

"What are you doin' with them ice cubes?" Clara was scandalized as she watched Jill bring Frank's hand into the bowl, pack the cubes about it.

"It's the newest thing for a burn," Frank explained. "I'm afraid the rear half of the barn is a total loss. We'll have to close in the good half, build it out again later. But Herb's studio area is intact."

"How did it happen?" Clara asked, lacing and

unlacing her hands.

"Who knows how a fire ever breaks out?" Frank shrugged. But his eyes were somber. "The storeroom's completely destroyed." Were all his books lost? But there must be a copy somewhere.

"Don says he'll be right out," Marian reported. "And he said to pack Frank's hand in ice," she added reluctantly.

The coffee began to bubble over onto the range. Clara moved to lower the flame, to hold the percolator aloft for a few moments while she mopped up the overflow of liquid.

"Coffee would be good right now," Frank said with a smile. "Cold out there, even if the temperature did shoot up fifteen degrees."

Frank, his hand settled in a bowl, moved to the table. Marian crossed to the window to report on the progress of the fire as Clara waited for the coffee to perk sufficiently to serve.

"Herb's sleeping all through this," Marian said with rancor. "Wouldn't you think he'd hear?"

"He took a pill," Frank explained. "He said all the dampness was bringing on his arthritis."

Clara poured coffee, brought the cups to the table.

"I'd better get upstairs. Mama'll be havin' a fit, not knowin' what's goin' on down here."

They heard a car pull up outside. Don, Jill guessed with anticipation.

He came directly into the house. Jill darted to the corridor, called out to him.

"We're in the kitchen, Don."

He praised her for her application of ice, and she glowed, watching as Don inspected the burn and applied medication.

"It isn't serious, though it might have been without the fast ice treatment." He looked about with a reassuring smile. Marian's own smile was painfully set.

Jed came in through the kitchen door, blowing against the cold.

"Fire's about out. They're hangin' around a bit to make sure it won't start up again. I figure they can use a little nourishment."

"I've made coffee," Marian said majestically.

"I've got somethin' that'll warm 'em up faster," Jed said with a grin. "A bottle of bourbon."

Twenty minutes later they heard the fire truck pull out. Mel and Jason joined the group at the table. Marian enjoying her role of hostess as she brought the percolator of coffee to them. Mel and Jason seemed exhilarated, Jill thought. They'd battled the elements and won. Again, she was conscious of Jason's tremendous personal magnetism.

"You're covered by insurance, aren't you, Frank?" Jason dropped himself into a chair beside Jill.

"For the structure, yes." Frank sighed heavily. "The contents of the storeroom, no."

"Were the copies of your novel in the storeroom?" Jill asked, suddenly alarmed.

"All hundred copies," Frank conceded. "Still in the carton in which they were shipped. I tried to get in there. I couldn't make it."

"You have another copy somewhere?" The book was out of print. It couldn't be bought from the publisher. "Frank, somebody must have one around."

"There may be one," Frank said tiredly. "Gil — my lawyer — asked for one when it was first published. To keep in my file. To him it was a kind of property. But after all these years, I doubt that he'll have it." He sighed with frustration. "That was thirty years ago, Jill."

Chapter Twelve

Jill woke up with a startling suddenness. Late, she realized. She pulled herself up on one elbow, squinted at the clock. Almost eleven!

Last night's drama flashed across her mind now. Nothing serious — except for the loss of Frank's books. Frank had dashed into the blaze to save that carton of books. They were important to him. Important enough to risk serious injury. How awful if his lawyer had discarded the copy in Frank's file!

She tossed back the covers, reached for the robe at the foot of her bed, crossed to a window that faced the Atlantic. The view this morning contrasted gloriously with last night's storm — the sea calm, the sun brilliant. Far out on the horizon a motor boat skimmed the blue water.

Don't stay indoors on a day like this. Dress. Get outside. Remember to ask Frank, when he comes home from the plant, if he'll check with his lawyer about that copy of his book.

In slacks and sweater Jill left her room and went down to the kitchen. Clara served breakfast informally on demand. Approaching the door, she could hear Marian talking with someone.

"I was thinking of something from Shaw,"

Marian was saying. "Frank liked that. Do you think your ladies would approve?"

"Oh, I'm sure they would adore it, Marian," Phyllis Lattimer said effusively. "You know how little culture we get up here."

Both women glanced up as Jill entered. They were annoyed at this intrusion, and their greetings were coolly polite.

"Sit down and I'll bring you breakfast," Clara ordered. "Sausages and eggs, hot popovers and coffee."

"Sounds fabulous, Clara. Oh, how was Mr. Danzig's hand this morning?"

"He didn't complain none. Went to the plant as usual." Clara took a plate from a cabinet, moved to the range. "Didn't have enough sleep, what with all the goings-on."

"I'm doing a show for Phyllis' club," Marian said as Jill settled herself at the table. "A one-woman show," she emphasized. Scared, Jill guessed with amusement, that Jill might try to become part of the act. "Frank asked me, and naturally I'm happy to oblige." Marian preened imagining herself performing before an audience the kind of roles she would never play in a professional theater. Jill was amused, but instantly felt guilty at her unkind assessment.

"Work out your program, Marian, and I'll have copies made up." Phyllis smiled sweetly at Marian. They had joined forces against the common enemy — Jill.

"Have you seen Mel's paintings?" Jill asked on

impulse. Remembering the art exhibit in the lobby of their tiny off-Broadway theater for the night of that one performance. "It might be interesting to have some paintings on display at the same time as the reading."

"Oh, no!" Marian's eyes glistened with rage. "Mel's paintings reflect the wrong mood to accompany my readings. They're harsh and ugly." She turned to Phyllis, deliberately cutting Jill from the conversation. "I'll have my program set up by tomorrow morning. That'll give you plenty of time, won't it, Phyllis?"

The phone rang. Clara picked up the kitchen extension.

"Hello." Her voice was querulous, as though she resented telephone interruptions. And then her voice brightened. "Oh, just a minute, Dr. Munson. I'll call her." Clara turned around. "Dr. Munson callin' you, Miss Conrad."

"Thank you." Self-consciously aware that all three women were listening, she picked up the phone. "Hi, Don."

"I promised three little girls in the hospital this morning that I'd bring a beautiful lady to read them fairy tales. Are you going to let me down?"

"I'd love to read to the little girls in the hospital," she accepted. What a lovely chance to see Don unexpectedly! "What time should I be there?"

"About three. Okay?"

"Great. See you at three." She put down the

phone, returned to her breakfast with a glow of anticipation.

She was relieved when Marian and Phyllis left her alone at the table. She finished breakfast leisurely, then headed for her room to collect her parka and to change into boots. Halfway up the stairs she encountered Jason in boots, faded Levi's, and a car coat.

"Get a coat and let's go for a look at the sea," he suggested exuberantly. "Days like this are rare in March."

"My thought exactly," she laughed.

"I'll ask Clara to give us a thermos of coffee and some sandwiches," he said.

"I've just had breakfast," she laughed. "I overslept. And I have to be back for an afternoon date. I'm reading to some children at the hospital this afternoon."

"Galahad's project?" He seemed faintly annoyed, Jill realized.

"Yes." She was defensive.

"Get your coat." He discarded any further thoughts he might have been about to expound on this subject. "I'll bring you back in time."

When she came downstairs, Jason was in the kitchen talking to Clara, who was making thick roast beef sandwiches for them. The thermos of coffee already waiting. Jason was Clara's pet. Of all Frank's guests, he was the only one for whom she had any genuine liking.

Jill and Jason left the house, circled around to the sea, down the treacherous flagstone steps that led below. The day a delicious harbinger of spring despite the cold.

Jason talked nostalgically about New York, yet she knew he was determined to remain at Cliff House for months. He was a disturbing man. He had a gift for making her feel naive. Still, it was exciting to be with Jason.

He was talking now about his ambitions, as they walked along the shore.

"You've got to be brash in this world. Take what you want. Playing within the rules," he conceded with a mocking bow. "But I'm so close to success now I can taste it, Jill. And it tastes great. I won't let anything stand in my way this time around." And then quite suddenly his conversation took a fresh route. "Jill, how do you think the fire started?"

"I can't imagine." Something in his voice commanded attention. "What do you think was responsible, Jason?"

"Herb could have been careless with that potbellied stove. He's a nut, you know. Lives in a world all his own. The only thing that bothered him this morning when he heard about the fire was that rotten sculpture of his. And how could that be damaged?"

"Frank says insurance covers the barn," Jill said. "But it's awful that his books were destroyed that way."

"Jill, knock off this business of Frank's novel," Jason said.

"Why?" They stopped walking.

"Because it's no good. He's built himself a nice, comfortable life. Don't push him back into that writing world again. He's going to bash his head against a stone wall."

"What makes you think he can't write?" Jill challenged. Her face hot.

"He's a tool manufacturer," Jason said. "He wrote one book thirty years ago. By accident he sold it. He told you, Jill. It sold eleven hundred copies. Any talent he might have had is atrophied by now."

"I'll let you know what I think about it when I've read his book!" Jill shot back. "You have no right to condemn him without reading it!"

"It'll be a lucky thing for him if he can't dig up another copy. Leave him in peace, Jill. Don't build up dreams in him again. He'll hate you for it."

"I'll take that chance. I'm praying he finds a copy of that book in his lawyer's file. And if it's good, I'll do everything I can to push Sheila into helping him!"

"Miss Pollyanna," Jason snapped. "What makes you think you know what book is good and what's bad?"

"I have an open mind, which is more than you can say." Tears of rage stung her eyes. "Suddenly I'm not in the mood for a walk anymore. You'll excuse me, won't you?"

She swung around, almost stumbling over the rocks in her haste to get away from Jason. He was furious with her. But no more furious than she was with him.

A few minutes before two-thirty Jill left her room, sought out Jed to ask for the keys to the Mercedes. For a moment she thought he was about to refuse, so she explained about the errand to the hospital. Frank would be furious if Jed disrupted Don's plans.

"I'll get the keys for you," he said sourly, crossing to a cabinet and reaching inside. "You be careful. That car's kinda funny sometimes."

"I'll be careful," Jill promised.

With keys in hand she decided to go back upstairs to change into warmer clothes. A sharp drop in temperature had been predicted. The sun, so beautiful earlier, was in retreat.

She changed, hurried downstairs and out to the garage. Jed was in the garage working on the pick-up truck. She forced a smile as she slid behind the wheel of the Mercedes. In the rear-view mirror she could see Jed standing at the door of the garage, watching her drive away.

She went over the directions to the hospital, which Jed had given her in detail. If she missed the right turn down the hill, he'd cautioned, she'd drive a mile and a half out of her way.

She watched carefully as she approached the right turn. There was the sign. "Spruce Hill." Make a right.

She turned right, started down the steep hill. Actually, this was the side of the mountain, she realized, reaching for the brake. She frowned. Her heart suddenly thumping. Her foot was down to the floor on the brake, but it wasn't responding!

She was going too fast! The car was out of control! Try the parking brake, her mind ordered. She reached frantically for it. Gripped it with all her strength. No good. It wasn't going to hold.

With terrifying speed the Mercedes was tearing down the mountainside. She had to stop! How? Her mind raced for a way to cheat death. Make a sharp turn at this wide spot. Now!

She braced herself for the crash into the clump of woods off the road. The Mercedes came to a grinding stop as it smashed against a giant tree trunk. Dizzy from the impact, but held snug by her seat-belt, Jill heard the crunch of metal at the contact. Miraculously, she was in one piece, she realized with giddy exhilaration.

She sat still for a few moments. Trying to quell the trembling that imprisoned her. But she was all right, her mind insisted. No broken bones, no cuts, nothing except this lightheadedness that would go away in a minute.

Don't waste time sitting here. Hitch a ride to the hospital. Tell Don what happened.

She pushed open the car door, stepped out into the wooded area. Steadying herself, because her head whirled with the effort to remain vertical, she forced herself to stumble out of the woods onto the road and gazed up the hill.

A car was coming toward her. She stood hopefully at the side of the road. The car slowed down. She recognized the driver. He was the man who ran the general store. He stared sharply at her, and released his brake pedal. He wasn't going to stop for her, and sped by.

She began to walk down the hill. According to Jed's directions it wasn't much more than a quarter of a mile to the hospital from this point. That was no walk at all.

Jill walked briskly, aware of stiffness, of soreness from the impact of the crash. Frank wouldn't be upset about the car, she knew, but he'd be distraught because she'd had another near-fatal accident. Why had the brakes failed? Had somebody tampered with them? *Who?*

As she approached the foot of the hill, she spied the hospital to the left. Unexpectedly modern. A low, sprawling, multiwindowed structure. She'd have to phone Jed, she realized with discomfort, so he could arrange for a pick-up of the car.

She walked into the cozy warmth of the reception room, through a pair of double glass doors. What a contrast to a city hospital — not even a nurse in sight.

Then a young nurse with an armload of fresh linens emerged from a swinging door, smiled at Jill.

"Could you tell me where I can find Dr. Munson?" Jill asked. "I — I'm supposed to meet him here at three."

"Wait a sec." The girl walked to the desk, leaned forward to push a button. "Dr. Munson, front desk, please. Dr. Munson."

Don — in a white jacket, unfamiliar to Jill — strode through a door to the right with a wide smile of welcome.

"Ah, my present for the children's ward," he said to the nurse, who watched them with friendly curiosity. "She's going to read fairy tales to pediatrics patients. I promised."

"I had some difficulty getting here," Jill said softly as they walked down a corridor in the direction of the ward. Her voice uneven with remembrance.

"What kind of trouble?" Don was suddenly tense.

"The brakes on the Mercedes gave out when I was coming down the hill. I was panicky — not even the hand brake would hold. I swung off the road to break my speed, crashed into a tree trunk." She smiled shakily. "The car's a mess, but I'm okay."

Don stopped dead. His eyes anxiously searched her face. He reached for her hand, as though to reassure himself that she was unhurt.

"Jill, you might have been killed!"

"But I wasn't," she said matter-of-factly. How upset he was! "Don, don't look so stricken."

"I want to see that car," he said. He, too, was suspicious. "Before you call Jed and he arranges to have it hauled in, I want a look at the brakes."

While Jill described the exact location of the car, a huge woman in white — her cap indicating she was the head nurse — strode toward them.

"Everything under control, Maggie?" Don

145

asked. Obviously there was a warm personal relationship between Don and the head nurse. But right now she wasn't looking at Don. She was staring at Jill. The color drained from her face.

"Who's your friend?" she asked brusquely.

"Maggle, meet the new aide for the children's ward. She's been drafted to read to the kids. Jill Conrad. Maggie Ryan, the best nurse this side of the Mississippi."

"Hello, Miss Ryan," Jill said softly.

"Everybody calls me Maggie," she snapped back. Her eyes fastened on Jill. "Where'd you find her, Doc?"

"She's a guest at Cliff House," Don explained. Maggie was upset. *Why* was Maggie upset? Why did so many people in town look at her as though she were a ghost?

"Must have been a shock to old lady Webster." The color was back in Maggie's face now. Her voice was almost natural.

"Why?" Jill asked swiftly.

"First time there's been a girl your age living in Cliff House since Denise died. Denise was the fairy princess of this town, and that house was her castle. Lots of us envied her, having everything the way she did. But we loved her, too. There was something special about her. My generation never forgot her."

"I'm going to introduce Jill to the pediatrics ward, then I have to cut out for about fifteen minutes. McTavish is around, isn't he?"

"Dr. McTavish is playing chess with Mr. Johnson in his private room," Maggie said with sarcasm. "We've got instructions not to disturb him for anything less than a massive coronary."

The children squealed exuberantly at Don's approach. None of them was seriously ill, Jill guessed with relief.

"Betsy has to be here with the leg in traction for another couple of weeks," Don said, rumpling the child's fair hair. "Donna goes home tomorrow — she's just here for observation. You won't taste any more bottles you don't know about," he said with mock sternness, and turned to Jill. "I got to her just in time. And Cindy here had a bout with pneumonia, but she's almost as good as new. We'll be turning her loose Monday or Tuesday."

"She looks just like a fairy princess," Betsy decided, gazing with delight at Jill, and Jill tensed. That was what Maggie Ryan had said about Denise Webster.

"I'm going to take a run out to the car now," Don said quietly. "Happy story-telling."

Jill was deep into the antics of an adventure story, when she glanced up and saw Don standing in the doorway.

"Five-minute break," he called out with a show of humor. "I'll send her right back, kids."

Amid good-natured protests Jill left the line-up of beds and moved out into the corridor to talk with Don. Her eyes anxiously seeking answers in his.

"There was no brake fluid in the car," he reported grimly. "There could be a logical explanation — some reason for the fluid leaking out. Or it could have been drained. By someone who knew *you* were taking the car out."

"Oh, Don!"

"Dr. Munson in emergency. Dr. Munson in emergency please!" A note of urgency in the feminine voice that called him. "Dr. Munson, please report to emergency!"

"I'll pick you up in about forty-five minutes," Don promised. "McTavish is on duty — I should be able to cut out to drive you home."

But at the end of forty-five minutes, it was the young nurse they'd encountered on their arrival who came in to Jill.

"I'm to drive you home," she explained apologetically. "Dr. Munson's scrubbing for emergency surgery."

Chapter Thirteen

Jill sat in the dining area of the kitchen, sipping hot coffee. A tight little smile about her face as she pretended to scan the local newspaper, which Clara had just set before her.

Clara was upset about the accident with the Mercedes. Her eyes kept moving to the kitchen door. She was waiting for Jed to return.

"Don't know why it's takin' Jed so long to tow the car in," she grumbled. "I don't know why he bothered," she emphasized. "He coulda called the garage man and *he* woulda gone out with the tow truck. Jed ain't savin' that much, bringin' it in himself."

"Something smells delicious." Jill strived to make casual conversation, in order not to think about those moments when the Mercedes charged down the mountainside out of control.

"I just put in the roast." Clara's voice was thin. "Can't figure out what happened to my baster. Can't find it anywhere." She pulled open cabinet doors, searching again. Banging them shut in frustration. "Who's been messin' around in the kitchen?" She stiffened to bird-dog attention. "That's Jed comin' back with the jeep."

A few minutes later Jed came in through the

kitchen door, red-faced with the cold. The earlier pre-spring warmth had been replaced by typical Maine-winter temperature.

"You stop by and tell Mr. Danzig?" Clara asked. Fleetingly her eyes moved to Jill with reproach. Clara was concerned with repair bills. Frank was covered by insurance, Jill thought defensively.

"He wasn't at the plant," Jed said reluctantly, and Clara stared at him.

"What do you mean, he wasn't there?"

"Just what I said," Jed snapped back. "I stopped by, and they said he'd left for the day. He'd been gone since lunch."

The phone rang. A discordant jangle in the supercharged atmosphere of the kitchen. With a frown on her face, Clara crossed to pick up the kitchen extension.

"Hello," she said sullenly, and then her face brightened. "Oh, hello, Dr. Munson. She's right here." Clara turned to Jill. "It's for you —" Jill moved hurriedly to take the phone, conscious that the other two were curious about the relationship between Don and her. Disapproving.

"Hi, Don."

"I'm sorry I had to cop out this afternoon. An emergency appendectomy came in. It couldn't wait."

"I understood, Don." A doctor's wife coped with endless emergencies. Dinners grew cold on the table. Social engagements were broken. Night sleep disrupted.

"Frank popped in about half an hour ago." He spoke so quietly now that Jill had to strain to hear. There was little privacy in the hospital, she guessed. "He came in so I could change the bandage on his hand — it was stained from grease at the plant. I told him about the Mercedes. He thinks it was an accident." Exasperation in his voice now. "Frank just doesn't want to accept the fact that these could be attempts on your life."

"I hope the children enjoyed the story hour," Jill said pointedly, because Clara was eavesdropping. Jed had gone out of the kitchen. Was he listening in on the phone in the library?

"Oh, you were a rousing success." Don followed her lead. "Will you come again?"

"Regularly," she promised. Don't think about a time when she might not be here.

"I'll try to call you later," he promised, and hung up.

Jill left the kitchen to go into the library. Jason was sprawled in a chair near the fireplace.

"Still sore at me?" The charm was turned on full wattage.

"No," she laughed.

"Let's play some chess," he suggested, forsaking his chair to head for the chess table. His eyes were oddly watchful. Had he heard the commotion in the kitchen when she'd come in and announced that the Mercedes was smashed up?

They were deeply involved in the first game when Jill looked up and spied Frank in the door.

151

A manila envelope under one arm. His face pensive.

"Hi." She smiled in welcome. "We didn't hear you drive up."

"You all right?" Frank asked anxiously.

"I'm fine."

"That's what Don said when he told me about the freakish accident."

"What kind of accident?" Jason demanded. "From what I overheard, I thought you'd just run off the road." He grinned at Jill. "I didn't ask questions — I didn't want to make you feel uncomfortable."

"The brakes wouldn't hold. Going downhill," Jill said. "I swung off the road and crashed to a stop."

"Thank God you kept your wits about you." Frank shook his head. "I left the plant early to stop off so Don could change this." He held up his bandaged hand. "I was awfully upset when he told me, Jill."

"Frank, don't worry about it," Jill urged. "I was lucky."

"Before I saw Don, I dropped by my attorney's office." He cleared his throat. "Gil had a copy of the novel in my file. After all these years. I have it here, if you still want to read it —"

"Of course I do." Jill jumped up eagerly to take the manila envelope Frank extended. "I'll read it tonight."

"After dinner," Jason stipulated with mock sternness. "Right now you're sitting down to this chessboard so I can finish beating you." But his eyes were serious. He was suspicious about those brakes.

"Don't be so confident," she answered Jason.

Frank left the room to wash up for dinner. Jill was pleased for him that the book, after all, was not lost. How marvelous that the attorney had held on to a copy!

Jason leaned back in his chair, gazed at Jill.

"You're going to sit down and try to read that book at one sitting," he guessed. "Then you're going to come downstairs and tell Frank how much you enjoyed it. How can you do otherwise?" he dared, "when you're living here in his house? Then he'll start to write again. You'll shake him out of his comfortable little groove and he'll never fit into it again."

Color flooded her face.

"How do you know the book isn't good?" How smug Jason could be! "You're taking a lot for granted!"

"It only sold eleven hundred copies," Jason reminded her bluntly. "And he's never written another line in all these years." He leaned forward intensely. "Be honest with him, Jill. Don't fill him with sad little ideas about how he's going to win a Nobel prize in five years."

"I intend to be honest," she said defensively. But if it was awful, how could she tell Frank? Now she was uneasy.

Immediately after dinner Jill went upstairs. In her room she settled in a chair beneath a comfortable reading lamp, kicked off her shoes, willed herself to relax. But from the first page of Frank's book she was swept into the story.

After fifty pages of reading she stopped to change into pajamas and robe. Impatient to be back with the book again. Delighted, as she returned to the printed pages, by the sweep of the novel. She read until her eyes began to close. Reluctantly she capitulated, abandoning the book for the night, and climbed into bed.

Oh, Jason was wrong about Frank's book. Wrong!

She awoke late in the morning, went downstairs for a quick breakfast, returned to her room to pick up Frank's book again. Relieved that she hadn't encountered any of the others downstairs. Eager to immerse herself again in the novel.

She was a compulsive reader, Jill acknowledged honestly — but there was a power in this book that she hadn't expected. She enjoyed the reading not only because the story was so engrossing, but because the reading was vindicating her impulsive prejudgment.

She ignored lunch to finish reading, then leaned back with a rich sense of satisfaction. How could this have sold only eleven hundred copies? Out of its time? This happened. Sheila had told her about a book that was revived in paperback thirty years after its initial printing, to receive fantastic critical acclaim.

Call Sheila tonight, she decided with a surge of excitement. Tell Sheila about this discovery. Perhaps Sheila could sell her company on bringing out a paperback reprint. Frank would be thrilled at a readership of paperback magnitude.

Later, when she knew Sheila would be home from the office, Jill went into the library to make a call to New York, relieved that the library was deserted for the moment. While she was waiting for the operator to put through the call, Jed walked in with logs for the fireplace and stared sharply at her.

"I'm calling New York collect," she explained, lest he believe she was charging long- distance calls to Frank's bill.

"Goin' home?" A glint of interest in his eyes.

"No. I'm just calling my roommate." She waited restlessly while he dumped the logs into the box beside the fireplace, picked a couple to toss into the grate. Why didn't he go out? Then she straightened to attention. Sheila picked up at the other end and the operator asked if she'd accept the collect call.

"Yes, I'll accept," Sheila was saying briskly, and Jed, finally, with reluctance, ambled from the room.

"Hi," Jill said exuberantly, and not stopping for small talk launched into the saga of Frank's book. "Sheila, it's terrific. It ought to sell tremendously in paperback. I couldn't put it down!"

"Send me a copy," Sheila instructed. "I'll read it right away. If it's as good as you say, I'll take it into the editorial meeting on Monday."

Jill waited impatiently for Frank's arrival, relieved that Jason was upstairs pounding away at the typewriter, that the others were watching television. Hearing the Bentley pull up at the entrance, she hurried down the corridor to the door and walked out into the night.

"Frank, I read the book," she said as he approached. "I think it's terrific."

"You read it already?" His eyes were eager for reassurance.

"I started last night, finished today. Frank, it's a fascinating book. I expected it to be good," she said with candor, "but I hadn't expected it to be *so* good."

Together they walked into the house, bound together with the pleasure of discussing the book. Frank, enjoying the depth of her enthusiasm, was astonished when she talked about the possibility of a paperback.

"Let me have several Xeroxes made," Jill persuaded him. "I'll ship one right out to Sheila — and you'll have the extras in case anything happens to the original when you return it to your attorney. Do you have a Xerox at the plant?"

Frank chuckled.

"We have an ancient mimeograph that fills our plant requirements. But there's a Xerox place about nine miles south. If you're sure you want to bother —"

"I'll drive over in the morning," Jill decided. "Just tell me how to get there."

"Jed will give you directions," Frank said, and then grew serious. "I've ordered a rented car until the Mercedes is repaired. It's supposed to be brought out first thing in the morning."

"Great." She smiled determinedly. All right, Frank wanted to believe the brake fluid leaked out by accident. Don't fight him on it.

"Would you please tell Clara that I'll be washed up in five minutes?" Frank headed for the downstairs bathroom. "I don't think Jed — or Clara — heard me pull up."

"I'll tell her."

She almost collided with Jed as she approached the kitchen. He was pulling on his coat, talking over his shoulder to Clara.

"I'll bring in more logs soon as I put away the car. Can't do everything at the same time," he grumbled. He *had* heard Frank arrive.

"Mr. Danzig asked me to tell you he was home," Jill said to Clara. What was Clara doing with that baster?

"I heard him," Clara said impatiently. "Only time I don't hear is when they're blasting down the road. Now why do you think some fool would come out to the kitchen and take my baster, then mess it up with oil? I can't clean it up," she decided with exasperation. "I'll have to throw it away and buy a new one."

Someone had used that baster, Jill suddenly realized, to withdraw the brake fluid from the

Mercedes. *Someone who wanted her dead.*

All through dinner Jill's mind focused on the tableau in the kitchen. Clara with the baster coated with what she believed to be oil. Brake fluid, Jill was sure.

Frank was in such a jubilant mood about the book. How could she tell him that here was proof that someone had drained the fluid from the Mercedes? She'd tell Don. Don would know what they must do.

"Don't tell me this is typical Maine weather," Jason was demanding of Frank. "It feels like early May."

"It won't last," Frank warned. "We had a taste of it the other day, now again today. We'll have plenty of snow before the flowers come up."

"Jill, let's take a walk along the beach after dinner," Jason suggested. Frank stared sharply at him. "You can't genuinely appreciate Maine until you've walked along the beach on a moonlight night like this when there's a breath of spring in the air."

"It's treacherous weather." Marian's voice was coated with distaste. Her eyes were angry as they settled on Jill. Marian was furious that Jason and Jill could appreciate a moonlight stroll along the sea. "But you can't tell young people anything — they think they know it all."

"We won't catch pneumonia," Jason promised. "Stop worrying about us, Marian."

Right after dinner Jason piloted Jill from the

dining room toward the stairs. He was anxious to erase the rancor of their last walk along the beach, Jill sensed. All right, she could forget that.

"Let's get our coats and cut out," he said briskly.

"Give me five minutes," Jill insisted. "I want to change into slacks." Remembering the dampness.

Jason was waiting for her at the front door as she hurried down the stairs, impatient now to be walking along the rocky stretch that flanked the sea. In silence they followed the path that led to the beach.

"Jason, how glorious!" Moonlight spilled over the slate-colored Atlantic, lending an eerie beauty to the waves and softening the austerity of the rocky shore. The lights of a ship far out to sea were visible in the fogless night. "It's like a marvelous painting."

"Come on, let's walk." Jason reached to take her hand in his. "You should have worn gloves." Unobtrusively she withdrew her hand.

"My pockets are deliciously warm."

They strolled along the edge of the water. Enjoying the scent of the sea, the promise of spring in the air. And then she stumbled unwarily. Jason reached to steady her. Unexpectedly he was pulling her close.

"No," she rejected softly. "I'm just getting over a bad thing, Jason. I don't want to jump into another."

His eyes were cynical.

"If it were Dr. Galahad, you wouldn't be so cautious. Come on," he ordered briskly. "Let's walk."

They walked in silence for a few moments. Jill was discomforted by the brief exchange. Was she so obvious about Don?

"What's this secret stuff between Frank and you?" Jason punctured the uneasy silence between them. "He was in such high spirits this evening. And he kept sending you silent messages all through dinner."

"It's his book." Here was impersonal territory. Safe for discussion. "It's far better than I expected." That jolted him. "It's terrific. About a sensitive boy growing up in a small Maine fishing village. And it's told with such vividness. Such poignance. I phoned my roommate in New York. She's a paperback editor. She's going to read it." Why was Jason glaring at her? "If Sheila agrees with me, she'll take it into an editorial meeting and try to have the book accepted for publication."

"You told Frank?" Jason's voice rose with incredulity.

"Of course —" What was the matter with Jason?

"You little idiot! Why didn't you wait to find out if your roommate agrees with you? She might think it's a piece of garbage! Do you realize how disappointed he'll be if there's no sale, after all your hoopla?"

"But Jason, the book's great!"

"That's your opinion," he reminded brutally. "Your friend's an editor. She's in a better position to judge. For God's sake, Jill, why couldn't you have waited and spared him another disappointment?"

Jason was absolutely psychotic about Frank's book, she thought defensively. It upset him that Frank might have this late success. And, he was furious with her for trying to bring it about!

Chapter Fourteen

As Frank had promised, a rented car was brought to the house early in the morning, while Jill was at breakfast. When she had finished, she asked Jed for the car keys. He looked sharply at her, shrugged, and handed them over. Did he expect another accident today?

En route to the Xerox service, she stopped off at a pay phone to try to reach Don. His answering service reported he was already making his house calls. Would she like to leave her name? Quickly, she declined. Don would worry if he received a call and then couldn't reach her. She'd phone again later.

In the Xerox shop the woman behind the counter made a note of Jill's order.

"Will I be able to have four copies today?" Jill asked. If she could send a copy off to Sheila today, the book would go into the editorial meeting on Monday.

"Oh, no," the woman said apologetically. "We couldn't get them out before Monday. We're backlogged."

"One set today?" Jill asked hopefully. "It's awfully important."

"Wait," the woman said sympathetically. "Let

me talk to my boss."

In a moment the woman returned.

"We can give you one copy in about an hour. We'll have the other three by tomorrow at two." She headed for the rear room where the Xerox machines were located.

Sitting down on a bench provided for waiting customers, Jill picked up a magazine to skim while the copy was being made. Her mind refused to cope with the printed words, and returned instead to the heated discussion with Jason about Frank's book.

Jason was wrong to be furious with her. She *had* to tell Frank. She didn't have the right to ship the book off to Sheila without Frank's permission.

With a sigh of exasperation Jill abandoned the effort to read, asked the woman behind the counter about a coffee shop in the vicinity.

"Two doors down," she instructed. "They make a fine cup of coffee."

Jill lingered briefly in the coffee shop, moved on to the small variety store next door. She shopped for several trivial items, all the while remembering — with discomforting vividness — how the owner of the general store in the village had refused to pick her up when he recognized her. Such hostility, she thought with a shudder. *Why?*

"The first copy's ready," the woman greeted her cheerfully on her return. "I'm just putting it into a box for you."

"Thank you."

Jill reached into her wallet. She would stop off at Chuck Travers' shop to buy wrapping paper, wrap the box and take it right over to the post office. Ship it out airmail special to Sheila. It would make the Monday morning editorial meeting, she decided with satisfaction.

Chuck was alone, sitting by the potbellied stove, an incongruous, if charming, touch in the sprightly modern shop.

"I hear you had a close call." His voice was solicitous.

"The brakes on Frank's Mercedes went," she explained, recovering from surprise at his knowing about it. But the garage man must have talked about it. The whole village must know. The realization was disconcerting.

"Had some trouble with poachers, too," Chuck remarked. He was unhappy about all this, Jill sensed. What kind of a case was he building up in his mind?

"That's right."

"Frank isn't having any trouble with that burned hand, is he?"

"No, he's all right." She couldn't bring herself to probe for his source of information. She held up the box containing the Xerox of Frank's novel. "I need some wrapping paper and a ball of cord for this."

"You don't need to buy cord or paper," he announced. "Let me have that. I'll wrap it for you. There're some address labels in the top drawer of my desk. Take one. Use my type-writer."

"The royal treatment," Jill laughed. "Thanks so much." But he *was* disturbed for her.

"Kate was quite impressed with you," he said as he pulled a length of brown wrapping paper from a roll.

"Kate Meredith?" All at once she was alert.

"Kate thinks you're very lovely, very bright." His face softened. "Kate's a rare person. Fiercely loyal to her aunt. She doesn't have much of a social life, tied down the way she is. Once in a while she allows me to drag her off to dinner and a movie. Frank contrives to bring her to Cliff House whenever he can. She has a right to her own life, but there she is, stuck, taking care of the old lady."

"I like her," Jill said impulsively. "I wish we could be friends."

The parcel wrapped, Jill left the gift shop, and walked down to the post office. "It should arrive by Friday," the postal clerk assured her.

Leaving the post office, she decided to try to reach Don. She was impatient to tell him what she suspected about how the brake fluid was removed from the Mercedes. She checked her watch hopefully. Perhaps she could spirit him off for lunch.

Don was walking out his front door just as she pulled up before the house.

"Hi. Can I shanghai you for lunch?" she said. She leaned out the window, saw his surprise. He hadn't recognized the car, of course.

"If you'll settle for Bill's," he said, striding toward the car. Delighted to see her.

"The car's a rental," she explained. "Frank had it delivered this morning."

"It has to be Bill's because I've got only forty minutes before my appointments start popping in," he explained, sliding in beside her. "Mrs. Sommers gets nervous if I keep them waiting more than ten minutes."

"Why not Bill's?" she agreed, but she hadn't forgotten her earlier visit to Bill's luncheonette.

"Old Bill doesn't serve Minnie's brand of food," Don warned her. "The fanciest thing you'll get there at lunch is a western omelet."

"I'll settle for a western." She reached for the ignition key. "Oh, about how the brake fluid was drained from the car," she said with calculated calm. "I think I know how it was managed."

"Tell me," Don said tensely.

She related the incident in the kitchen with Clara.

"Anybody in the house had access to that baster," Don said slowly.

"Which does narrow it down, doesn't it?" But her heart was pounding. "It couldn't have been an outsider."

"Don't narrow it down," Don warned her. "We don't know who might have slipped into the kitchen. Someone familiar with Clara's working schedule. Don't narrow it down."

They drove in silence for the few blocks to

Bill's. Inside a sprinkling of diners lingered at the counter. The four tables, with their much washed tablecloths, their slender vases, a single pink paper rose in each, were deserted. Most of Bill's luncheon business for the day was over. Bill sat at the end stool, reading a newspaper. He glanced up as Jill and Don walked in. Again, his eyes fastened on Jill. With an effort he pulled his gaze away from her, nodded to Don, and pretended to be very busy behind the counter.

"A pair of westerns, Flo," Don said as the waitress moved from behind the counter to their table. But he was aware of Bill's reaction to her presence, Jill knew. His eyes were grim, belying the casualness of his voice. "And coffee now, please."

"As if I didn't know, Doc," Flo drawled. "Coffee coming up."

Don leaned forward, speaking very quietly.

"I see what you mean about Bill. You really throw him."

"I told you."

"We've got to do some digging around, Jill. Explore this secrecy."

"How?"

"I don't know yet." He frowned in thought. "Let me think about it." His hand reached out to hers. "I'm not letting anything happen to you, Jill!"

When Jill heard Frank's voice in the foyer, she hurried downstairs. She reported her activities with the book.

"It's a miracle to me that you like the book," Frank said. "That you're interested enough to try to do something with it. After all these years of feeling my talent was worth nothing."

"I think it's a terrific novel," Jill insisted.

"Talk, talk, talk," Jason drawled behind them. His tone was good-natured, but his eyes clashed dangerously with Jill's for a moment before they settled on Frank. "How's everything at the plant?" Frank often brought home humorous vignettes to report at the dinner table.

"I was a total loss at the plant today," Frank admitted. "Couldn't keep my mind on business. Did Jill tell you what she did with my novel?"

"I told him," Jill said swiftly. Don't let Jason make some cynical remark.

"I sat there at my desk, and my mind just boggled with the possibility of having maybe a hundred thousand paperback readers sharing that book with me. I kept thinking about all those notes I've piled up through the years. Cartons of them." The new exhilaration in him touched Jill. "And I wondered if I could sit down and write again."

"What are you going to write, Frank?" Marian trailed behind them into the dining room, with Herb at her elbow. Jill caught the angry glance bestowed, fleetingly, on her.

"I've planned a trilogy," Frank confided with new openness. Mel stared stonily at Frank from his chair at the dining table. Herb stood frozen, as though startled at the prospect of Frank's resuming a writing career. "For years I've sat and plotted out scene by scene each of three books. I've made all those notes. I know every character as well as I know myself. I know how they think, how they react, how they feel. The dialogue is all there in my mind. The characters have been my daily companions for twenty years." He chuckled. "It's as though I have a movie projector in my mind. I can play any scene from memory. I've just never put it down on paper."

Jill leaned forward earnestly.

"Let me type up your notes, Frank. I'm fairly fast and I'm accurate."

"I don't know, Jill," he hedged. His eyes were serious, hesitant. He was willing to talk, but fearful of committing himself. "Let's wait and see if your editor friend is as enthusiastic as you are."

"But in the meantime let me at least start typing up the notes," Jill coaxed. "Frank, I'll enjoy it."

"What's this about Jill's friend and the book?" Marian's smile was overly bright.

Jill turned inquiringly to Frank. He nodded.

"I sent it to my roommate, who's an editor at a paperback house. If she likes it —" Jill took a deep breath, glanced involuntarily at Jason, "and I'm sure she will, she's going to try to persuade her firm to publish it."

There was an outbreak of slightly hysterical

excitement from Marian and Herb. Mel looked cynical. Jason skeptical.

"May I start typing up your notes?" Jill said again when the excitement subsided.

"All right," Frank capitulated. "I'll dig out the first box tonight, leave it for you on the library desk before I leave in the morning. It's an insane amount of notes," he warned.

"Is there a spare typewriter around the house?" Jill asked with satisfaction. "Or do you have a spare at the office?"

"There's one in the unused wing. Tell Jed to bring it out and set it up wherever you like." He glanced about the table as Jed began to serve. "Marian, I thought of something this afternoon. Why don't you do a run-through of your one-woman show here at the house for us, before the performance at Phyllis' club? A sort of preview."

"I don't know —" Marian pretended to be reluctant.

"On Broadway, when a show can't go out of town," Jill said diplomatically, "they preview."

"Yes, I could do that." Jill saw the glint of approval in Marian's eyes.

"Next week, the way things are going, I should be finished with the statue," Herb announced, his eyes moving triumphantly about the table. "I'll have to do something about finding a home for it." His eyes rested hopefully on Frank. But Frank had withdrawn from table conversation for a private discussion with Jill about his notes.

Jill saw the rage on Herb's face when he realized Frank was oblivious to his remark. "Frank —" Herb raised his voice sharply. "Do you know anybody who might be interested in my statue?"

"I'll ask around," Frank said absently, and Herb's eyes settled vindictively on Jill.

Jill forced herself to concentrate on the roast beef Jed had placed before her. Uneasy beneath Herb's rage. Aware, too, that Jason was annoyed with her for pushing Frank into writing again. Wow, she had a knack for stirring up hostilities!

They were just leaving the dining room when Don phoned.

Self-consciously, she hurried ahead of the others to take the call in the library. Faintly breathless, eager to talk with Don, she picked up the phone.

"Hello."

"Jill, can you meet me at the office tomorrow about three?"

"Sure, something special?" The others were coming in behind her now. She wouldn't be able to talk freely. Don knew about the extensions. He'd be guarded in what he had to say.

"We're going to do some visiting," he said carefully. "It might prove interesting."

"Fine," she said with an effort at lightness. "See you then." Where was Don taking her? What did he expect to discover? She wished that they could have talked more freely.

Earlier than normal Jill said good-night, left the library to go up to her room. Inside her room, she shut the door, crossed quickly to the windows to shut the drapes. Her eyes were drawn compulsively to the single grave below, tonight shrouded in the fog that was moving in from the sea.

Why did people in this town look at her as though she were some terrifying intruder? Maggie Ryan. Mrs. Webster. Hallie, the cleaning woman. Bill at the luncheonette. The man from the general store looked at her with hate, because she was from the city, she decided. That was a different ballgame.

Somebody in this town wanted her dead, or at least to frighten her into leaving. Enough had happened to convince her of that. Why did Frank persist in shutting his eyes to this fact? She wasn't being hysterical. *Somebody wanted her out of the way.*

All at once chilled, Jill left the front windows to close the drapes at those overlooking the sea. Before the hour passed, visibility would be zero. She could hear the poignant blare of a foghorn somewhere in the distance, calling the boats in to shore.

Try to read a while. Despite her tiredness, she knew she wouldn't fall asleep right away. Not with her mind so active.

She stooped before the fireplace, lit a match, and put it to the crunched-up newspaper stuffed between the birch logs, laced with kindling wood.

She stood up, waiting for the kindling to catch

on, absorbed for the moment in this small task. Pleased when the kindling began to crackle, knowing the logs would soon catch and burn far into the night.

She took out her pajamas and changed before the lovely comfort of the fire. Then chose a book from the collection of paperbacks atop the chest.

But in bed, tucked cozily beneath the covers, with the fire crackling heartily, she gazed at the first page of the book without seeing a word. Her mind focused on that brief phone conversation with Don. Don was alarmed for her safety. While she found comfort in this, his anxiety also intensified her own.

Eventually she felt herself drifting off to sleep. She deposited her book on the table and reached to switch off the bedside lamp. Grateful for the russet glow that suffused the hearth, she turned her face to the fireplace and fell asleep.

Jill awoke reluctantly. The room was in complete darkness. No light from the fireplace. She tugged the blankets snugly about her shoulders against the sharp night chill from the sea. And then, suddenly, terror shot through her.

She stiffened, hearing the heavy breathing somewhere in the room. *At the fireplace.* She started at the faint clink of the shovel. Someone was covering the logs with ashes, to blot out all light.

She couldn't lie there, waiting for him to attack. *Do something.* Fearful that her anguished breathing would give her away, she noiselessly turned down the covers, slid her feet to the floor, reached for the book on her night table. Flung it through the blackness, toward the fireplace.

She heard the muttered oath as the book struck its quarry. Then something whizzed past her, and she screamed.

She ducked to the floor. Hearing the screams pour from her throat. Hearing the door to her room close. *But she'd locked the door last night.*

She fumbled for the lamp, found it. Switched it on with trembling fingers. Turning to the wall behind her, she paled when she saw the chisel imbedded in the plaster. The chisel would have killed her if she hadn't chosen just that moment to reach for the book.

She struggled into her robe, slid her feet into slippers.

"Jill!" Frank was knocking frantically at the door. "Are you all right?"

"Yes, yes," she called out, hurrying to the door.

"Frank, what is it?" Marian's voice. High. Near hysteria. "Who screamed?"

"Jill, I think. But she's all right, Marian," Frank was saying as Jill pulled the door open. "Perhaps a nightmare."

"Somebody came into my room." Jill's breathing was painful. She was conscious of Jason and Mel striding down the corridor. Herb would sleep through anything when he took one of his pills. But the chisel was the one Herb used on his statue. "Whoever it was, threw a chisel at me." She shivered. "He missed by inches." She pushed the door wide, nodded toward the chisel imbedded in the wall.

"That was an attempt at murder." Jason was angry. "Frank, you'll have to call the police."

"I'll call them," Frank sighed, "but let's wait a while. The chief gets up at five anyway. Jill, I'm sorry." His voice was anguished.

"Where's Herb?" Mel demanded.

"Probably fast asleep," Jason surmised, and strode down the corridor to Herb's door. He knocked. There was no response. Impatiently he tried the door. It was locked. "He was complaining last night about his arthritis, with all that fog. He probably took a pill. He'll sleep till late in the morning."

"Who could have done it?" Marian's contralto was unnaturally shrill. "Somebody wants to kill us! Who's going to be next?"

"The villagers hate us," Mel said with contempt. "They think we're a bunch of freaks."

"I can't understand why anybody would try to harm Jill." Frank's face was gray. "What motive could there possibly be?"

"When we find the would-be killer, we'll know," Jason said. "Jill, why didn't you lock your door?"

"I did." Why couldn't she stop trembling? "I'm sure I did, Jason."

"All you need is a plastic card to open any of

these doors," Mel pointed out dryly. "That's no problem."

Frank turned anxiously to Marian.

"You'll catch cold standing out in the hall this way. Go back to bed. Would you like me to bring you up some hot milk? It'll help you get back to sleep."

"How can I sleep after this?" Marian demanded dramatically.

"Mr. Danzig?" Jed's voice, filled with alarm, drifted up to them. He stood at the foot of the stairs, buckling his belt. "What happened up there?"

"An intruder, Jed," Frank explained. "Please go into Miss Conrad's room and remove that chisel from the wall."

"Anybody hurt?" Jed was nervously climbing the stairs.

"Nobody hurt," Frank said, frowning. "Just get that thing out of the wall, and go on back to bed."

"Miz Henderson sleep through it?" Jed asked as he reached the top of the stairs. "Clara sleeps through anything, but most times her mother knows if somebody sneezes anywhere in the house."

"Mrs. Henderson may have taken something for her nerves." Frank fought to conceal his irritation over this chit-chat. "She didn't hear anything." He glanced about at the somber faces of the others. "Let's all go down to the kitchen and have something hot to drink. It's chilly in the

176

house at this hour. I'll make coffee, and we'll wait till five to call Tim Roberts."

"You can wait," Mel said sourly. "I'm going back to bed."

"You'd better go to bed, too, Marian," Frank urged again gently. "If you catch laryngitis, there'll be no performance for Phyllis' club."

"Perhaps you're right, Frank," Marian accepted shakily. "I am susceptible to night chill. I'll go to my room." She turned to Jill. "I hope you have enough sense after tonight to leave Cliff House."

Jason frowned, reached for Jill's arm.

"Come on, Jill. Let's go down to the kitchen and see how good Frank is with a percolator. While you're putting on the coffee, Frank, I'll start up a fire in the kitchen."

"Go on down and start the fire. I'll just go back to my room for a moment to put on socks," Frank said apologetically. "My feet get cold, I'm cold all over. I'll be right downstairs."

"Afraid to go downstairs alone with me?" Jason challenged. "Do you think I crept into your room and tossed that chisel?"

"Of course I'm not afraid," Jill answered quickly.

But who did toss that chisel? It could have been Jason. It could have been anybody in this house. Or someone from the village who'd crept in through a door or window left carelessly unlocked.

She shivered, remembering that anguished

moment when panic had almost overtaken her. When she knew she was not alone in her room. Realizing, that a would-be murderer had stood but a few yards away.

Chapter Fifteen

Sharply at five Frank called Tim Roberts, the police chief, on the kitchen extension, while Jill and Jason sat sipping their third cups of coffee. Logs piled extravagantly high in the fireplace, sending warmth across the room. The first light was showing in the sky and the morning heat hissed in the radiators.

"I'll explain when you get over here, Tim," Frank said with a rare edge of sharpness in his voice, in reply to Chief Roberts' questions at the other end. "Come right over," he added in a more conciliatory tone, "and I'll coax Clara into making us a good breakfast when she comes downstairs."

"It's deliciously warm down here now." Jill tried to sound in control. Wishing she could get rid of the feeling of living in a nightmare.

"It's a shame we can't get the heat upstairs this way," Frank said. Taking refuge, as she was, in small talk. "I've had all kinds of work done on the furnace, but it never gets up to scratch. But the fireplaces help, don't they?" He looked from Jill to Jason.

"The fireplace in my room is great," Jill nodded earnestly. "I love watching the firelight as I fall asleep." But two hours ago someone crept into her room and banked the fire into darkness. She shivered, her mind assaulted by ugly recall of those moments.

"Why don't we all go upstairs and dress?" Frank suggested. "If you'd rather dress somewhere else, Jill, there's the room at the end of the corridor that I haven't redone yet —"

"I don't mind going in there now," Jill said quickly. But she did. "Jed pulled out the chisel — and it's almost daylight." Don't let Frank know how sick she felt at the prospect of walking into that room again.

In record time the three of them had dressed and returned to the kitchen. Frank and Jason stood by the fireplace in low-keyed conversation when Jill walked in, changed to slacks and yellow cashmere sweater. An air of tension in the kitchen because momentarily Tim Roberts would arrive. The murder attempt would be a matter of public record.

"I've put up another percolator of coffee," Frank said, as Jill moved to join them at the fireplace. "It'll be ready in a few minutes."

"I think I saw the first crocus coming up," Jill reported. Searching for safe conversation. "Just the tips."

"They're about due," Frank agreed. "We have masses of them out front."

"What's everybody doin' in the kitchen at this hour?" Clara's voice swung their attention to the door. "I got up early because Mama woke up aheada schedule and asked for her coffee. What's everybody doin' down here?" She looked anxiously at Frank. "You feel all right, Mr. Danzig?"

"I'm all right," Frank reassured her, but she still seemed worried. "We're waiting for Tim Roberts to show —"

Clara paled.

"What's Tim Roberts doin' out here this time of mornin'?"

Succinctly, his voice showing strain, Frank explained the situation. Clara shook her head in disbelief. As Frank finished, they heard a car pull up outside.

"I'll go let him in," Clara said flatly. "Then I'll put on some bacon and eggs. Can't be talkin' about somethin' like this without food in your stomach."

Jill crossed to sit down at the table. Dreading the encounter with Tim Roberts, though Frank made good-humored fun of their local police chief and his three-man force. While she fidgeted in her chair, Jill could hear Tim Roberts and Clara talking as they came down the corridor to the kitchen.

"I don't know what's goin' on," Clara was saying as they arrived at the kitchen. "You'll have to ask Mr. Danzig about that. I just walked downstairs and there they all were. At this time of mornin'."

Tim Roberts was a short, massive-shouldered, beer-bellied man in his fifties, who took his job

181

seriously. Jill guessed he shared the villagers' distaste for Frank's city guests. His eyes lingered skeptically on Jason and her as Frank introduced them. While they were explaining what had happened in the night, Clara rattled pans with more than customary vigor. Her hand must have slipped with the lavender bottle, Jill thought with fleeting amusement — Clara reeked of the scent this morning.

"How many other guests you got here right now?" Tim Roberts pulled out a chair, dropped clumsily into its comfortable breadth.

"Three others," Frank said.

"Better have 'em come on down," Tim said briskly.

"They're upstairs sleeping, Tim," Frank said testily.

"I gotta question them, Mr. Danzig," Roberts pointed out.

"What can you ask them?" Frank countered. "We were all asleep in our beds when we heard Jill scream. We all ran out into the hall at the same time."

"Now, Mr. Danzig, it's part of procedure," Roberts said. "I gotta question everybody in the house."

"Come back this afternoon and question the others." His voice took on an authority new to Jill and Jason. His plant voice, Jill decided. "It was an outsider, Tim."

"How do you know that?" Roberts pounced. "You see anybody?"

"I saw nobody." Frank was struggling not to lose patience. "But I saw the others come out of their rooms. They'd all just been awakened by Jill's screams. Talk to the three of us now. Come back this afternoon and talk to the others. But mainly, Tim, you look around in the village to see what you can find out. I can vouch for my guests," he said firmly as Clara came over to set an oversize mug of coffee before Tim Roberts.

"All right then —" Tim paused to take an appreciative swig of coffee, then pulled a notebook out of his pocket. "Let's try to pin down who — outside of the house — would want to kill the girl."

Tim Roberts was sure it was an inside job, Jill realized. One of the guests. How unreal, to be sitting here, discussing her would-be murderer.

"I don't suppose you'd consider sending everybody back where they came from?" Tim asked. "That would make real sense."

"Nobody's leaving." Frank's eyes said he considered this a personal affront.

"All right, Mr. Danzig," Tim soothed. "Just thought it might make it easier all around."

"Tim, I want you to find out who sneaked into the house and threw that chisel." Frank's face was tight with frustration.

"Mr. Danzig, it's not going to be easy," the police chief warned. "First, let's go upstairs and get that chisel. We'll have to check it out for fingerprints."

Frank's face showed his shocked realization of

the futility of this.

"I'm afraid I ruined that for you," he apologized. "I sent Jed in to pull the chisel out of the wall. It must have Jed's prints all over it."

"That won't help none," Roberts said. "But we'll have to check it out for ownership, anyway."

"We know that. That is, we assume it belongs to a guest." Frank sighed. "He's a sculptor. The chisel was out in the barn, where he's been working. And that's unlocked. Anybody could get in there and take it."

"Herb was asleep when the chisel was thrown at Jill," Jason said with deceptive softness. He wanted to cut down the police chief for suggesting that the guests be shipped home. "Herb takes a pill for arthritis on these damp nights. He's out cold for ten hours."

Tim Roberts sat for another forty minutes throwing questions at them, eating Clara's fluffy scrambled eggs and crisp bacon. The toast was slightly burnt about the edges this morning, to Clara's annoyance. Only Tim displayed any relish for food at this hour, though Jill made an attempt for Clara's benefit.

Tim shook his head over the lack of leads. Feeling terribly important, Jill thought with impatience. Why didn't he finish up and get out of here? When he returned this afternoon, she remembered, she'd be away from the house. With Don.

"More coffee, Chief?" Clara came toward him

with the percolator. "Before I go upstairs to check up on Mama."

"Don't mind," he said calmly. "And fill it up to the top." One of Clara's niceties was to leave an inch for cream. "I drink it black."

Jill leaned back with relief when Tim Roberts sauntered off with a self-important swagger. She was tired from lack of sleep, yet too unnerved to go upstairs to take a nap as Frank had urged earlier. It was comforting to sit with Frank and Jason in the bright, attractive kitchen. The early morning sunlight was beginning to sneak in through the curtains, making last night seem a bad dream. Almost.

Frank glanced at his watch.

"I'll have to leave in another ten minutes."

"You're going to be bushed," Jill said apologetically.

"I don't need a lot of sleep." But he looked exhausted. "Would you like Clara to open up another bedroom for you? There's one that isn't really much to look at — I haven't got around to fixing it up the way I'd like — but Clara keeps everything clean."

"I don't mind staying in my room," Jill said quickly. "If I could just get a stronger lock on the door." She blushed. She shouldn't have said that, she thought guiltily.

"I'll have Jed put a bolt on the door today," Frank promised. "I'll tell him before I leave for the office."

The three of them at the table froze to attention at the sound of a car pulling up out front. Jason, frowning, rose to his feet. "I'll go see who it is."

Jason strode down to the corridor to the door. Searching for conversation, Jill mentioned the Xerox copies she'd be picking up later. She was anxious that Frank return the original to his attorney's office.

"Jill —" Frank hesitated, choosing his words. "If nothing happens with your friend in New York, don't be upset. I want you to know how much I appreciate your trying. Your interest."

"Frank, I've told you — I think it's a terrific book. It's a disgrace that you haven't written all these years."

Jill looked up just as Don walked into the kitchen with Jason. He grew serious as he listened to Jason repeat the events of the night. His face became taut with shock.

"I stopped in at Bill's for coffee," Don said, his gaze focused on Jill. "The cop on the dayshift was there. He told me there'd been some trouble out here. I jumped right into the car and came out."

"If she hadn't moved just when she did," Jason said bluntly, "we'd be holding a wake for her."

"Sit down and have a real cup of coffee," Jill urged. "I'll get it for you —" Don was shaken, she realized with a rush of tenderness.

Jill poured coffee for Don and herself. Both Frank and Jason demurred.

"I'll have another at the office," Frank said.

"Mattie feels my day hasn't started until she's brought me coffee." He pushed back his chair with an air of reluctance. "This is one day I'd prefer to stay at home, but it's a bad time of month to take time off."

"Nothing's going to happen to me in broad daylight," Jill reassured him gently. "Don't worry, Frank."

"What did Tim Roberts come up with?" Don asked.

"Knowing him, what would you expect?" Jason said with contempt.

"He's not a sophisticated big city detective." Frank was annoyed at Jason's bluntness. "His training is limited." Frank got up. "I'd better head for the office. I'll tell Jed about the bolt," he said, turning to Jill with a reassuring smile.

Jill hoped that Jason would decide to go upstairs, but he seemed determined to out-sit Don. Don finished his coffee, rose briskly, his eyes in brief communication with Jill's. No chance to talk now, with Jason here.

"I've got to take off for hospital rounds."

While Jill framed words to take her to the front door with Don, Jason adroitly circumvented her intention by holding out his cup. "Jill, I'll have coffee now."

"All right." She would see Don at three. She would wait till then to talk with him.

After still another cup of coffee, Jill went upstairs to try for a nap. She was exhausted. Actually, she had nothing to do until it was time to drive over to pick up the Xeroxes. After two, the woman had said. Pick up the copies, take the original to Frank at the plant, and then drive over for Don.

At her door she paused. Her heart pounding. Reliving those frightening moments of last night. Hearing the heavy breathing in the blackness. The zing of the chisel as it sped past her to imbed itself in the wall behind her.

But that was last night. Nobody would come sneaking into her room in broad daylight. And some time during the day Jed would put up the bolt. *Nobody would get in tonight.*

Jill forced herself to open the door. To walk into the room. Her eyes moved to the bed. The covers were thrown back as she'd left them this morning, when she'd dressed swiftly, impatient to be out of the room.

She closed the door behind her, crossed to the bed, sat down at the edge, kicked off her shoes. Oh, she was tired! She stretched along the length of the bed, sighing as she adjusted her slender frame to a comfortable position.

How good it felt to lie down. She closed her eyes, giving herself up to tiredness, and dropped off to sleep within minutes.

Jill awoke with an instant realization that she had slept for hours. What time was it? Anxiously she lifted herself on one elbow, leaned forward to inspect the clock on the bedside table. Nearly two! She'd have to rush to pick up the copies.

She rose swiftly, took out a car coat from the closet. Don't stop to eat. Grab a sandwich at a diner along the road. Right now, she recoiled from a face-to-face encounter with the others in the house. Could the police chief be right? Had someone at Cliff House thrown that chisel at her?

Walking down the corridor to the stairs she could hear Marian rehearsing in her room. Jason was typing. Mel was listening to the radio in his room. Last night might not have happened. Except the wall behind her bed bore the grim imprint of that chisel.

She went to the kitchen for the car keys. Clara wasn't there. Jed was at the table, having cake and coffee. He glanced up with a mixture of sullenness and caution.

"Jed, may I have the car keys?" Trying to sound casual.

"They're right there on the hook." He nodded toward the far corner of the kitchen. His eyes not quite meeting hers.

"Thank you." She collected the keys, hurried out the kitchen door and cut across to the garage.

What did Jed think about last night? Could it have been Jed in her room? He showed up at the foot of the stairs minutes after the chisel came whizzing toward her. Could he have run down the stairs in that time, and then showed up in the foyer? No! Don't try to guess! Wait and talk about it with Don.

She slid behind the wheel of the rented car with a sense of escape. For a little while she was running out on the danger that seemed to hang over her head.

As she drove out of the garage, her eyes inspected the winter-gaunt grounds. Down the driveway, at the barn, the workmen were hammering lumber into place. And then her gloved hands tightened on the wheel. She felt a dryness in her throat. Even at this distance she sensed the anger in Herb as he stood at the barn door, watching her approach.

"Hi." She waved, striving for casual friendliness.

Herb waved back, swung about awkwardly, and walked into the barn.

Jill drove past the grave of Denise Webster, down the long route to the main road. Remembering Mrs. Webster's voice as she complained to Kate about Frank's bringing *her* to Cliff House.

There were so many threads that ought to be tied together. So many suspicions pricking at her consciousness. But don't worry about those things now. For a little while this afternoon be just a girl on a vacation in Maine.

A girl with a rendezvous with death? No! Don't believe that. *Don't believe that.*

Chapter Sixteen

Jill stopped briefly at a roadside luncheonette for a sandwich and coffee, then headed for the town where the Xerox service was located.

The woman at the service greeted her with a broad smile.

"We have the copies waiting." She reached for the boxes beneath the counter, handed them over with the bill.

Jill hurried back to the car, checking her watch. As she'd planned, she'd be able to stop by the plant, drop off the original of Frank's book before she met Don. Frank said his attorney would be at the plant today. She'd feel better with the original back in the attorney's files.

Now she allowed her mind to focus again on what most disturbed her. No use playing games with herself. Whoever tried to kill her last night — and the other times — would try again.

Sheila would say, "Pack up and run!" Sheila had a logical mind. But she didn't want to run. She wanted to stay here. Near Don.

Stay. Walk a tightrope. Find out who was trying to kill her. Find out *why*. So many loose ends. Together, Don and she must try to slide the jagged pieces into one clear picture.

At the plant Mattie greeted her with warmth.

"He's with a customer," Mattie told her. "But I'll tell him you're here." Her eyes were lively with interest. No doubt remembering the day Jill had picked up Frank for lunch, Jill realized uncomfortably.

"No, I wouldn't want to disturb him," she said quickly. "Would you please make sure he gets this?" She extended the envelope that held the original of his book. "It's important."

"I'll be sure he gets it," Mattie assured her.

Jill drove directly to Don's office. Mrs. Sommers was gone for the day. Don sat at his desk, head in his hands in concentration.

"What, no patients?" she asked flippantly. "I thought I'd have to tear you away from the office."

"Mrs. Sommers cleared the afternoon for me. I sat up till all hours last night, Jill, trying to figure out what was going on." Jill had noticed how tired he looked. "And while I sat here thinking, somebody zapped that chisel at you."

"They missed." Again, striving for a lightness she didn't feel.

"Let's go over to Bill's and have coffee." Don rose and reached for his coat. "Then we've got some calling to do."

Jill was conscious of Bill's start when he caught sight of her. Don noticed, too. He waited until after Flo had taken their orders to talk about it.

"Question One," Don said quietly. "Why do

you upset the old boy? He's not sharp enough to hide it. Maggie turned white the first time she saw you. Why?"

"Don, I can't figure it out," Jill said with frustration. "All this keeps churning around in my mind, but I haven't come up with any answers."

"Jill, what about your family? Could they have ever lived in this area? Perhaps when you were a small child? Could the people here know you?"

"No one in the family ever set foot in Maine," Jill protested. "Not even on a vacation."

"When we leave here, we're going over to talk to Chuck. He's supposed to be an authority on the history of this town. Maybe we don't want to go back to the Revolutionary War days," he conceded with a laugh, "but Chuck might be able to dig up some useful facts."

They drank their coffee, left the luncheonette, and went into the gift shop. There Chuck, who greeted them as long-lost friends, listened with shock to the account of last night's near-tragedy.

"You think the smash-up with Frank's Mercedes was rigged, too?" Chuck asked uneasily.

"I'm sure of it," Don said. "Since the day Jill set foot in that house, somebody has been plotting to kill her. The question is, who? Someone inside the house — or someone outside?" Don sighed. "Chuck, we've got to get to the root of this thing. I don't expect much action from Tim Roberts."

"It's almost as though history were trying to

repeat itself," Chuck said morbidly. "Denise all over again."

"Was Denise Webster murdered?" Jill asked softly.

"I didn't mean that." Chuck was flustered. "I meant that for the first time in forty years someone of Denise's age is living at Cliff House. And again tragedy threatens."

"Chuck, give us the whole story," Don suggested. "I've heard it in bits and pieces. But what actually happened?"

"Denise was about eighteen, as I understand it. She was going to be married in a month. She was leaning out a window, calling to her dog down on the beach — and she fell. Denise had a mentally disturbed brother, Todd, who was about fourteen at the time of her death. Afterward, he had to be institutionalized."

"Chuck, did her brother have anything to do with her death?" Jill asked.

"Actually there were ugly rumors at the time. People hinted that Todd had pushed Denise out the window. But Clara worked in the house at that time and she said that Todd was with her in another room when Denise fell. He couldn't have been responsible. I understand he'd been deeply upset at the prospect of Denise's getting married." Chuck looked from Jill to Don. "Did you know that Denise was engaged to Frank?"

"Oh, no," Jill whispered. "Poor Frank."

"It's Frank who sends the red roses every year, on the anniversary of Denise's death. Secretly because he's a private person," Chuck said gently. "But how does this tie in with what has been happening to Jill? How could there be any connection between Denise's death and these incidents?"

"I'm working on instinct," Don paused to think. "There has to be a connection."

"If I can help in any way," Chuck said, "let me know."

"Don, what do you think?" Jill asked when they were out in the street again. "That someone in the village, someone connected with Denise's death, wants me dead, too?"

"I'm not ruling out anybody," Don said. "Inside Cliff House or out. But I think we've got to go back to Denise's death, search for some tiny clue that'll put us on the right track. I'd like to go digging in the old newspaper files, but if we did that, it would be all over town in two hours."

"What about going to a neighboring community?" Jill suggested. "Some place where nobody knows either of us. A murder would be reported in newspapers in neighboring towns as well."

"Jill, you think straight." He reached for her hand and squeezed it in approval. "We'll drive over to Brennan. It's a large enough town to have a decent newspaper, and nobody there knows us. Let's just hope their files go back for forty years." A note of apprehension crept into his voice.

"Let's go find out." Jill forced a smile of optimism.

"It would save a lot of searching if we had an approximate date of Denise's death," Don pointed out as they pulled away from the curb, "but I don't quite see us going to the house to inspect the inscription on her tombstone."

Jill was cold all at once, despite the fact that the heater flooded the car with warmth.

"I know when she died, Don. The day I arrived Jed said it was the fortieth anniversary of her death."

Her voice faltering, Jill repeated the date of her arrival at Cliff House. Remembering the man at the grave. The red roses in the snow. Frank standing, hatless in the near-zero weather, his eyes focused on the shattered roses, their petals strewn about the snow like blood. Without being conscious of it she had known then that Frank had loved Denise Webster.

"Let's get over to Brennan," Don said briskly. "Let's hope they have a newspaper that goes way back — and that they keep back copies for all the years."

"They'll probably have it on microfilm," Jill guessed. "Even small towns do that now."

"Honey, they won't have microfilm in Brennan," Don predicted. "If they have editions on file, they'll date back to the actual period."

"What are we looking for?" Jill asked after a moment. "Specifically what, Don?"

"I don't know," he said with honesty. "I expect to see some tiny item that'll lead us on to another, and we'll hope to get a complete picture. Just instinct." He grinned. "Some nerve, for a man of medicine to work on hunches. But sometimes," he went on whimsically, "a hunch leads me to a right diagnosis."

They were approaching a fork in the road. Jill pushed down the brake pedal.

"Which way, Don?" The signs were oddly rigged.

"To the left," he said after a moment. "I know the right goes to Richfield."

"To the left then." She swung off onto the other road. A tightness in her throat. What would they find in the newspaper files?

"When we get there," Don cautioned, "we don't ask specifically for the date we want. I'm a novelist searching for background material for a new book. I'll ask for newspapers in that particular month, over a span of five years."

"I'll remember."

They drove in silence for the next few miles until they approached the small Maine town that was their destination. A replica of Frank's town, Jill thought, but probably three times as large in population. The stores here wore a more aggressive air. There had been an effort at modernization.

"Let's park over there," Don suggested. "Then we'll ask around about the newspaper office."

Don went into a drugstore, bought a magazine, inquired about the local newspaper.

"Sure we got a newspaper," the drug clerk said

with pride. "Comes out every Thursday. They got their office right off Main Street. At the corner of Elm. It's the little white house next to the hardware store."

They walked with nervous haste from the drugstore to the newspaper office, paused a moment outside the eighteenth-century white house that carried a sign announcing, "News-Herald."

They walked up the steps, crossed the porch. Don pulled the door wide for Jill to enter, followed her. A girl at the desk in the foyer looked up at them with a bright smile.

"Hello." Don turned on his impressive charm. "I'm a writer, up here for the weekend. It's such a delightful town I've decided to use it as background for my next book. I'd like to do some research on this area, going back about forty to forty-five years. Would you have newspapers on file for that period?"

"Oh, we go back before the Civil War," the girl said with pride. She pushed back her chair, rose to her feet. "Wait here a minute. I'll go ask Mr. Kendrick to help you."

The girl disappeared down the corridor, returned shortly with a small, spry elderly man.

"You a writer?" The man squinted near-sightedly at Don.

"That's right."

"My name's Kendrick. I'm in charge of the records." He was debating, Jill guessed, about whether to make the effort to help them.

"I understand you go back to the Civil War," Don said with an air of grave respect.

"Before the Civil War." He smiled in decision. "What years you want?"

"From 1929 through 1934. If it isn't too much trouble, Mr. Kendrick."

"No trouble at all," Kendrick said with satisfaction, "for someone who can put it to good use. Don't like dragging out material for crackpots. You go sit in there —" He pointed to a room off the foyer. "And I'll send out the papers you want. When you get through with them, give them to Madeline here."

"Thank you!" Don smiled brilliantly.

Jill and Don walked into the room off the foyer. It held a desk and a pair of chairs. Don dropped into the chair behind the desk, made a show of pulling out a pen and a notebook, aware that the girl at the desk was watching them. In a few minutes a teenager ambled into the small office to deposit an armful of newspapers, divided by years, onto the desk.

"They're kinda crumbly about the edges," the boy said apologetically, "but all the issues are there."

"Thanks so much." Jill smiled in gratitude while Don reached eagerly for the pile of yellowing newspapers.

Don waded through the collection of newspapers, drew forth the vital week. Jill made a pretense of scanning another newspaper. Don held the one that should carry the story of Denise

Webster's death.

"Jill!" She reacted sharply to his almost immediate gasp of astonishment. "Right here on the front page!" His voice was muted because the receptionist said barely twenty feet away. He thrust the newspaper toward her. "Look at that photograph of Denise Webster."

Jill took the newspaper. Stared, disbelieving, at the photograph as she realized why Don had been so astonished.

Denise Webster might have been her identical twin.

Chapter Seventeen

"*I can't* believe it," Jill whispered. Staring at the replica of herself. "Don, what does it mean?"

"Let's get out of here where we can talk."

Briskly, because he knew the girl at the desk was curious about them, he made a pretense of jotting down notes in his notebook. Then he gathered together the pile of yellowing weeklies, stacked them neatly, and pushed back his chair.

"Okay," he said quietly to Jill. "Let's go."

He returned the newspapers to the girl at the desk, politely thanked her for her assistance, and moved with Jill toward the front door. They walked to the car in silence. With a sense of urgency. This time Don slid behind the wheel.

"Don, what does it mean?" Jill asked again.

"It means that somebody is disturbed because a dead-ringer for Denise Webster is living in this town again," Don said.

"Somebody who murdered her?" Jill's heart was pounding.

"We don't know that she was murdered," Don pointed out cautiously as he pulled away from the curb. "But let's work on the assumption that she was. Forty years ago, let's say, somebody pushed Denise from that attic window. Now you walk into town. That person, living with guilt all these years, could be pushed over the borderline of sanity —"

"Don, could it be Todd?" Jill interrupted. Todd, who was mentally disturbed. Who had to be institutionalized after his sister's death. "Perhaps Todd escaped from that institution and is hiding here in town?"

Don was quiet for a moment. Jill's eyes searched his face. Conscious of the tension in him.

"Don?" she said tentatively.

"Jill, I didn't say anything when we were talking to Chuck. I've never told this to anyone because I respect Mrs. Webster's desire for secrecy — and I don't have the right to discuss a patient with anyone else." For an instant his eyes left the ribbon of road to turn to Jill. "Todd was never institutionalized. That was the story concocted because he fell completely apart after Denise's death, and it would have been the logical thing to do. But he's been kept at home all these years. He lives in a room at the cottage, with his mother and Kate taking care of him. That's why Kate came to live with her aunt. He'd become too much for Mrs. Webster to cope with alone."

"Too violent?" Jill asked.

"Difficult," Don parried.

"Don, could he escape from the cottage from time to time?" Long enough to make those attempts on her life.

"Impossible," Don said emphatically. "His windows are barred. That's the reason for the high fence across the back of the cottage. Also, he's constantly sedated. Dr. McTavish and I look in on him at regular intervals. I was brought in when McTavish was away on a hunting trip, at a time when Todd's medication was proving ineffective — and his mother was desperate. But no, I can't see Todd getting away from the cottage. Besides, he was in no way responsible for Denise's death. At the investigation Clara said that she was with Todd in another room on the floor at the moment Denise fell — or was pushed — from the window."

"Clara *said*," Jill emphasized. "How do we know she wasn't protecting Todd? A fourteen-year-old mentally disturbed boy might have aroused her sympathy. She was close to the Websters. Don —" Jill leaned forward earnestly. "Suppose Todd saw me — disturbed as he is, he might look at me and think I was Denise, still alive. And now he's trying to kill her again —"

"We must consider that," Don acknowledged, but his eyes were skeptical. "No, Jill, I can't see how Todd could make repeated escapes from the cottage. Not sedated as he is. Not with his mother and Kate constantly watching him."

"We're going to have to go back forty years, and start from there." Jill gazed soberly into space.

"That's just what we're doing," Don said.

"We're driving over to visit a patient of mine."
He grinned. "She's been very unhappy because I
haven't had a steady girl. I'll bring you along to
show her the situation has changed." He
removed one hand from the wheel to touch Jill's
briefly. "Mrs. Magnani has lived here since she
came to this country over fifty years ago. She's
pushing eighty. Her eyesight's not good so I
doubt that she'll notice the resemblance to
Denise. But I have a hunch she might fill us in on
some details."

"What kind of details, Don?"

"I don't know." He shrugged. "We're playing
this by ear."

They pulled up before a modest little gray cottage with jaunty yellow shutters. Its chimney
belching forth smoke. Silently they left the car,
walked to the door. Don reached for the old-
fashioned knocker and banged sharply.

"The door is open," a surprisingly firm voice
with an Italian accent called out. "Come in,
please."

They walked into a small, low-ceilinged living
room, dominated by a Franklin stove. In an armchair before the stove, a basket of knitting in her
lap, sat the elderly but indomitable Rose
Magnani, showing no ill effects from her recent
stroke. Her face lit up with pleasure as she recognized Don.

"Doc Munson. You bring someone with you
today," she said slyly. "Is about time." She
nodded in vigorous approval.

"This is Jill Conrad, Mrs. Magnani," Don introduced. "From New York. But I think she likes Maine."

"Bella!" She leaned forward, beckoning Jill closer. Beautiful girl!" She smiled broadly. "You pick good, Doc Munson."

Mrs. Magnani didn't see the resemblance to Denise Webster, Jill realized. She hadn't reacted at all. But then the old lady's eyesight was failing, Don had said. "I've been bragging to Jill about what a great memory you have," Don said casually, while they seated themselves in chairs close to the Franklin stove at Mrs. Magnani's urging. "I'll bet you remember forty or forty-five years back with no trouble at all."

"I remember," Mrs. Magnani said with pride, "when I was a little girl living near Taormina."

"Do you remember when Bill opened his luncheonette in town?" Jill asked out of left field. Running on instinct.

"Oh yes, I remember." Mrs. Magnani nodded. "Maybe forty or so years ago it was. The old man — that was Bill's father — had been talking a long time about going into the restaurant business. A crazy man," she chuckled. "All the time he liked to cook."

"Bill's father opened the place?" Don was studiedly casual.

"With Bill. One day he told Mary, his wife — they're both dead now, God rest their souls — that he was through with farming. A quiet one he was. Nobody knew he had that kind of

205

money salted away."

"Where was Bill working?" Jill asked.

"Oh, he was a yardman," Mrs. Magnani said with good-natured contempt. "No more than twenty-one or twenty-two then. He worked over at the big house. For the Websters."

"Don, everything that's been happening to me has to relate in some way to Denise Webster," Jill said, when they were in the car again. "How was Bill's father able to open a restaurant that way? Not from money he saved farming! Because Bill was a yardman for the Websters — and the Websters paid him to be quiet about something!"

"You think Bill knew something about Denise's death?"

"He worked for the Websters. Maybe he was gardening below, looked up — and saw Todd push Denise."

"Something's amiss, Jill." Don insisted. "I can't believe that Todd could be responsible for these attempts on your life."

"Who else knows about Todd's living in the cottage?"

"Dr. McTavish, Maggie Ryan — that's about it. Oh, and Hallie, who comes in to clean once a week."

"Hallie owns a small cottage at the edge of town." Signals were jogging up in Jill's mind. "Clara is just a bit envious about that. Clara once mentioned that Hallie's had the house for about forty years." They were getting close to an answer! What was the missing part of this puzzle?

"I wonder what Clara did before she went to work for Frank?" Don said. "Let's go back to talk to Chuck. He knows the case histories of everybody in town."

Jill agreed and they headed back to the gift shop.

Chuck greeted them with curiosity. "You're on to something."

"We're not sure. We think so." Don proceeded to brief Chuck on their suppositions.

"Chuck, what did Clara do before she went to work for Frank?" Jill tried, futilely, to recall some hint dropped on this subject. There was the gap from the time she worked for the Websters until she came to work for Frank.

"You know she worked for the Websters at the time of Denise's death. Not long after she left town with her mother. Was gone for about four or five years, I understand. Her mother's a hypochondriac — you know that, Don."

"I know," Don acknowledged with a faint smile.

"Clara took her mother to doctors down in Boston. Even to New York. Then finally they came back here and settled down. She was busy taking care of her mother for the next few years, until Frank bought Cliff House. Then, of course, she went to work for him. I guess her money was short by then."

"All that running to doctors must have been awfully expensive," Jill said thoughtfully. "Was Clara's mother well fixed?"

"Not particularly. She was a widow from the time Clara finished high school." Chuck stared from Jill to Don. "You think Mrs. Webster paid off Clara, too, to be quiet about Todd? Assuming, of course," Chuck interposed conscientiously, "that Todd did murder Denise."

"I believe it," Jill insisted vigorously. "And now Todd's out to murder me. Thinking I'm Denise."

"No," Don denied again. "Not Todd. Someone who's scared to death your presence in town — your resemblance to Denise Webster — will drag the whole incident out into the open again. Hold it up to fresh light. Somebody who has benefited from keeping silent. You know they're all guilty of withholding evidence, if Todd did kill Denise and they knew it."

"Except that nobody, so far, has proved it was murder," Chuck reminded them.

"Remember what I heard Mrs. Webster say to Kate?" Jill swung to face Don.

Chuck leaned forward intently.

"What did she say to Kate?"

"She said —" Jill took a deep breath, seeking to recall Mrs. Webster's exact words. "She said, 'Kate, you saw her! Why did he bring that girl here? What is he trying to do?' "

"You've got a lot going for the theory that Todd murdered Denise," Chuck conceded.

"But where do we go from here?"

"Jill's driving me back to the office to pick up my car before she goes home. Then I'm heading for the hospital to ask some questions of McTavish and Maggie Ryan. I want some straight answers."

"Don't forget, you're both due at Cliff House for dinner tonight," Jill reminded. "Afterward, Marian's doing a preview performance of her one-woman show."

"Keep your eyes open at the house, Jill." Chuck's voice was serious. "You and I may be wrong in thinking it's Todd who's out to kill you. Don could be wrong in suspecting one of those who may have been paid off to keep quiet. Your would-be murderer could be sitting down to dinner with us tonight."

Chapter Eighteen

Jill sat tense behind the wheel. Her mind assaulted by flashes of Denise Webster's face. The resemblance between them was weird. Chilling.

"Jill —" Don's voice was uneasy.

"Yes?"

"After what happened last night, I don't like your going back to Cliff House."

"Don, I'll be all right." How could she sound so confident?

"Why don't you pack a bag and let me take you over to Richfield. There's a little hotel there. It's not fancy, but it'll be safe. We're so close to a breakthrough, Jill. Let's not take chances now."

"Frank told Jed to put a bolt on my door." Jill struggled to sound calm. "I'll be all right. And when I'm not in my room, I'll make a point of being with at least two people. I can swing that, Don," she added because he looked so distraught. "Nobody will try anything in front of witnesses."

"You'd be better off at the hotel," Don said bluntly.

"I'd be scared to death," Jill said honestly. "Alone in a strange hotel. And how do we know I might not be followed?" Jill shook her head resolutely. "I'll stay at Cliff House and I'll be careful."

Jill left Don at his office, drove — with mounting apprehension — back to the house. As she approached Cliff House, a car swung out of the driveway. Tim Roberts was leaving. He must have been questioning the others. Did he learn anything of value?

She put the car into the garage, walked to the house. Entering the foyer, she saw Marian standing in the doorway to the front sitting room. She was talking indignantly to Herb.

"The nerve of the man, asking us all those personal questions!" Her eyes swung accusingly to Jill as she became aware of Jill's presence. "He actually believes somebody in this house threw that chisel at you! He stated it blatantly! Not you, Herb," she said, consoling him. "Everybody knows you sleep through the night when you take one of your pills. Your doctor can vouch for that."

"I'm sorry Chief Roberts bothered you all that way," Jill said unhappily. "But Frank felt he had to be notified."

"It was my chisel." Herb's face wore a frightened expression. "I left it out in the barn. They're not going to try to blame it on me, are they?"

"Of course not," Marian said firmly. "If they were, he would have taken you with him." She closed her eyes dramatically for a moment. "I'm so upset that I don't know if I can do the performance tonight."

"Of course you can," Herb insisted. Being upset had not diminished his admiration for Marian's talents. "We're all looking forward to it."

Halfway up the stairs Jill heard a door open. Jason walked into view, carrying one of the copies of Frank's novel.

"You were right," Jason said flatly. "It's a terrific book. How could Frank have lived all these years with this kind of ability and not use it?"

"Jason, he's never stopped writing," Jill protested. "He has those cartons of notes, but never had the nerve to put them in novel form again." If it weren't for the chisel incident last night, she would have been typing up Frank's notes today. "He'll be at work again. You'll see."

"That'll be the end of Cliff House," Jason predicted. His face taut. "He won't need this mausoleum anymore." He sighed and added, "I hope Frank can handle this resurgence of his writing career."

"Why shouldn't he be able to handle it?"

But Jason was striding past her, intent on returning the copy to the library.

Jill hurried up the stairs, impatient to be behind the security of the bolted door of her bedroom. Breathless — from anxiety rather than exertion — as she arrived at the top of the stairs, she hurried to her door, pulled it wide.

She stared, disbelieving, at the inner side of the door. *Jed had not put on the bolt.*

She shed her coat, put away her purse, headed with mounting anger for the lower floor. Marian and Herb were still in the sitting room. They were talking in muted tones against the higher than necessary volume of the television set. She hurried out to the kitchen, intent on facing Jed. Frank had given him orders to install that bolt!

"Where's Jed?" she asked Clara with a forced nonchalance.

"He's down in the basement. Still working on the furnace. He's been at it all day. The house has been like an iceberg till an hour ago. Didn't you notice?"

"I've been out all afternoon." Couldn't he have taken ten minutes off to install the bolt? Or didn't he have one? How long would it have taken him to drive into the village to buy a bolt? Couldn't he understand how important it was?

"What do you want with Jed?" Clara asked.

"Nothing important," she evaded. "I'll ask him later."

Before Clara could question her further, Jill swung about and hurried upstairs to her room. She would put a chair under the doorknob. If anybody tried to get in, she'd scream loudly, enough to bring the others running.

In her room she positioned the chair against the door. Though it was dubious protection, she was determined to do what she could to prevent a possible intrusion.

She was tired. Her body ached from tension. A hot tub would be relaxing. She viewed the chair at the door with a tug of insecurity. But at this time of day there was too much traffic on the stairs for anything to happen to her. Run a tub, soak in water fragrant with bath salts. This was supposed to be a festive evening.

She let water run into the tub, lit the fire laid in readiness for the night. Jed had taken time out from working on the furnace to take care of the fireplaces. Why hadn't he taken the few minutes needed to attach the bolt to her door? Didn't he want a bolt on the door?

Don't think about that, she ordered herself. Relax this little while before dinner. Don was talking to Dr. McTavish and Maggie Ryan this afternoon. Perhaps he would come up with some constructive answers.

She left the door to the bathroom wide as she lay in the soothing, perfumed water. Unable to unwind despite her determination. Watchful for some slight sound that would indicate an intruder.

She dressed leisurely after a lengthy deliberation about what to wear. A long dress and costume jewelry to create a feeling that this was an occasion. To deny her taut nerves.

A car drove up outside. She moved swiftly to one of the front windows. Chuck was arriving. He hadn't stopped off to pick up Kate. Wasn't she coming? Did Kate's absence have anything to do with Todd?

When would Don come, she wondered impatiently. He hadn't called after he'd seen

McTavish and Maggie Ryan. But perhaps he hadn't done so because it was dangerous to talk over the telephone. He would come tonight, wouldn't he? Don's arrivals were fraught with uncertainty, being dependent upon the state of his patients' health, the situation at the hospital.

Jill took a final inspection of herself in the mirror. Everything seemed so unreal. Last night, the chisel zinging past her to lodge in the wall. Today, the newspaper photograph of Denise Webster. All the fresh facts about Todd Webster, about the conspiracy that might be surrounding him.

Go on downstairs. Push the chair away from the door and go down to the library. Phyllis Lattimer is arriving now. She's talking with Frank in the foyer. Nothing is going to happen with so many people around.

Jill was at the foot of the stairs when the phone in the library rang. She quickened her steps. Perhaps it was Don.

Frank peered out into the corridor, instantly spied her.

"Jill, there's a call for you."

"Thanks, Frank." Jill sprinted down the corridor and into the library. She picked up the phone expectantly. "Hello."

"Hi, Jill." It was Sheila, in high spirits. "I received the manuscript nine o'clock this morning. I stayed home because of a sore throat, so I figured I might as well read it right away. I read it straight through. Jill, it's a tremendous book. Didn't he ever try for a paperback?"

"The book just died after the initial printing, Sheila." Jill's eyes moved to Frank, who had stopped dead in the middle of a sentence as the identity of her caller broke through to him. "That was about thirty years ago, when paperbacks were just beginning to get a foothold."

"I called my boss," Sheila continued breezily. "She sent a boy over to pick up the manuscript. She read the first three chapters and called me back. She thinks it's great. We're going in to the meeting Monday morning to try for a sale, with a big promotion. With both of us fighting for it, Marcia's sure of a sale."

"Sheila, that's marvelous! Frank will be delighted." Everyone in the library was unabashedly eavesdropping.

"How are you? Having fun? Meet anybody interesting?" Sheila asked.

"Yes, Maine is beautiful." And ominous.

"You can't talk," Sheila guessed.

"That's right." Relieved that Sheila understood.

"Write me what's doing," Sheila ordered. "And I'll buzz you on Monday about the results of the meeting."

"That was my roommate," Jill said to Frank as she put down the phone. Her face aglow with satisfaction. "Sheila and her boss both like your book tremendously. They're going in to an editorial meeting Monday to try for a paperback contract. With both of them pushing so enthusiastically, Sheila feels it's fairly sure to go through."

"Well, how about that," Jason drawled. "We have a future celebrity for a host."

"Not a celebrity — a possible paperback writer," he said, trying to restrain his obvious delight.

"Sheila wants them to go in for heavy promotion," Jill added. "Frank, that paperback is going to put you right where you belong," she prophesied. "Among the important writers of this generation."

"Come in to dinner," Clara ordered from the doorway. "Before that roast beef gets all dried out."

Everyone headed for the dining room. Phyllis fluttering over Frank as she discussed the unexpected interest in his novel. Mel sullen about this sudden success of Frank's. Marian and Herb oddly wary, as though their trust in Frank was diminishing. Jason, walking at the tail of the procession with Jill, was cynically amused at these reactions, missing nothing.

"Oh, Jill." Frank halted just inside the dining room. "I forgot to tell you. Don's tied up with a patient. He may not get over at all this evening."

It was past midnight when Chuck and Phyllis left in their respective cars, and the others went up to their rooms. Marian was exhilarated by the warm reception to her mediocre performance. Jason was withdrawn, as he had been much of the evening. His recognition of Frank's talents unnerved him, yet, Jill suspected, gave him a fresh impetus to complete his own book.

Jill walked into her room with an acute awareness of her vulnerability. She should have told Frank this evening that Jed hadn't put on the bolt! Why *hadn't* she told him? Frank was so quietly efficient. He would have dug up a bolt from some place, put it on himself if necessary. She was just too upset these days to think logically.

Her eyes swept about the room, cataloguing its contents. What could she put against the door that would be more substantial than a chair? Something that would deter a would-be murderer.

The dresser. Could she manage to drag that across the room, shove it against the door?

Comforted by the sounds of voices out in the corridor, she changed swiftly into pajamas and robe. Now, she ordered herself, move the dresser.

She tugged speculatively at one end. The dresser was heavy, awkward — but she could manage. The realization sent a charge of relief through her.

Slowly she pushed the dresser toward the door. Noiselessly. Feeling guilty because the dresser left a trail on the carpeting. But the carpeting would not be damaged, she promised herself. She could raise the nap in the morning when she'd moved the dresser back — and nobody would know the difference. Right after breakfast she'd tell Frank that Jed had neglected to install the bolt.

There, slide the dresser around against the door. Firmly into place. Panting slightly she stood back to view the dresser's position. Nobody would be able to push through the door, she decided with shaky satisfaction.

By the time she was ready to climb into bed, the house was night-still. But once beneath the covers, she was wide awake. The room in unbroken blackness because the logs laid for the night fire had been consumed earlier. Lying against the pillows, she listened to every small sound in the night.

The rain that had been threatening all evening began to fall. In moments it was pounding against the windows. And the waves below beat against the rocks. Why hadn't Don called? She moved restlessly in bed.

Eventually she fell asleep. Into chaotic, terrifying dreams. Waking with a sense of plummeting through space. Fully awake in seconds. *Because the doorknob was turning.*

She tossed back the covers. Slid her feet into slippers. Reached with trembling hands for her robe. Whoever was on the other side of that door was discovering the block.

"Who's there?" she demanded impetuously, rushing to the door, her courage motivated by the presence of the dresser. "Who's there?"
And suddenly she knew.
In the dark she fumbled for the wall switch,

found it. Light replaced the darkness. With impatience she shoved the dresser away from the door. Caution ignored, she was intent only on a confrontation with her would-be murderer.

Breathless from the exertion of moving the dresser, she stepped into the corridor with impatient swiftness. As she came to the head of the stairs, the front door was closing. She sped down the stairs, pulled the door wide, and ran out leaving it open in her haste.

She darted out into the dark, stormy night. Hurrying after the figure perhaps thirty feet ahead —

Chapter Nineteen

Jill raced through the dark, hardly conscious of the cold rain that whipped about her with March fury. Intent on catching up with the figure lumbering ahead. Running dangerously along the edge of the cliff. Too caught up in the discovery of her would-be assassin to remember the perilous drop onto the crags below, washed now by angry waves.

"Wait!" she cried out in the night. Her voice echoed eerily in the stillness. "Wait!"

She was narrowing the distance between them. Her throat constricted painfully with the effort. Lightning flashed across the sky now, spotlighting the figure ahead. Jill, youth on her side, was catching up. In moments she'd be able to reach out to touch.

"Wait!" she ordered urgently. "Wait!"

"No." Suddenly the night-shrouded figure spun around. The scent of lavender oppressively strong. "You stay right there."

In a sudden flash of lightning Jill saw the knife in Clara's hand. The blade gleaming in the brightness. Ready to be plunged into Jill at the least provocation.

"Clara, why?" Jill asked. Her voice high with

disbelief. "Why do you want to kill me?"

Clara's face wore a strange, terrifying exhilaration.

"I'm going to kill you, the way I killed *her*. She was going to marry him. Why did she have to have everything? Even Frank! And now you come here to take Frank away from me again! I been with him for thirty years. Runnin' the house. Takin' care of him. Then you come back to remind him of *her*, who's been dead all these years. And then you started with the book. He'll go down to New York and he'll stay there. I'll lose him!" Her voice rose shrilly. "Because of all your doin's. Thirty years of takin' care of him — and I'll be left with nothin'!"

Keep Clara talking. Pray that somebody would hear them. Clara's voice was shrill with hysteria — it would carry in the night.

"Then Todd didn't kill Denise!" Let somebody be awake. Let somebody hear. "All the time I thought it was Todd."

"That's what I made 'em think." A note of triumph in Clara's voice. But she was edging Jill backward. Back to the edge of the cliff.

Don't think about those rocks below. Don't think about Denise, who died down there.

"How did you do that, Clara? How did you arrange it that way?" Keep talking.

"I walked into the room. She was standin' at the window, talkin' to that stupid dog down on the beach. Todd was hangin' around. He was always hangin' around her. I walked into the room, and I pushed her out the window." A flash of lightning dropped a stark white light about her face. "Todd ran to the window screamin' to her. Bill was outside. He saw Todd. I knew he'd figured Todd did it. Hallie came runnin' in from the hall. She thought Todd did it, too. Todd went crazy. Screamin' and carryin' on. He was never quite right." Clara's voice was oddly sing-song. "I told 'em Todd pushed Denise out the window. Bill saw Todd's face right there after she fell. The old lady paid us all off to keep our mouths shut. She didn't want Todd bein' dragged off to jail. Maggie Ryan came in to take care of him for a while — till Dr. McTavish figured out how to keep him quiet with all them needles. Mrs. Webster didn't want folks in town knowin' he was with her. She told everybody he'd had a breakdown because of Denise's death — and had to be sent away."

"How are you going to explain my death, Clara?" Jill's throat hurt with the effort to speak. She started at the sound of a twig snapping close by. Clara didn't notice. Was it some small animal — or had someone at the house heard them? "They'll find out. They'll put you away, Clara."

"Nobody's gonna put me away," Clara shot back. The steel of the knife in her hand gleamed in the darkness as she inched forward, moving Jill toward the edge of the cliff. "You're going to die. The way she died!"

"Clara!" Don's voice rang through the night. Moving closer. "Clara, wait!"

"No!" Clara shrieked, trembling with rage. "You won't stop me now! Nobody can stop me!"

Clara lunged forward toward Jill. Jill dodged, managing to avoid the gleaming steel. Clara lost her footing. Stumbled. Fell, screaming, to the rocks below.

"Jill! Oh, Jill —" Don pulled her back from the edge of the cliff.

"Don, I was so frightened!" Jill clung to him.

"You're all right, Jill. You're all right. The nightmare's over," he whispered, cradling her in his arms.

The rain descended with torrential force. Lightning crackled across the sky. But neither Jill nor Don was aware of them.

Except for Herb, who had taken a pill, Frank's guests sat with Don around the table in the dining area of the kitchen while Frank waited at the range for the coffee to perk.

They heard the ambulance, whose crew had removed Clara's body from the rocks, and the police chief's car driving away from Cliff House. Jed was outdoors throwing ashes on the walk because the rain had turned into a heavy snow-fall.

"Lucky for Jill you were returning from a night call," Jason said quietly to Don. "Lucky you looked up and saw the light in Jill's windows and heard Clara's voice in the night — and guessed what was happening."

"Luck had nothing to do with it! I was not just

224

passing by, I was trying to check the grounds. Since I couldn't get over to see Jill earlier, I thought I would come in if anyone was still up and see that all was calm. When Dr. McTavish told me that he was sure Todd could not have managed any of the threats against Jill, I tried to figure out logically who could. Once I thought of Clara's place in all of this, the answer was obvious."

Jill was trying, a bit shakily, to put it all together. "Then Mrs. Webster bribed all those people years ago for nothing. Todd did nothing except go further over the edge into his own madness."

"What a strange woman Clara was. She never demanded anything — seemed content, in fact. To murder out of jealousy and yet not ever insist on anything more than living here as my house-keeper —" Frank shook his head, a deep sadness seemed about to overwhelm him.

"What will happen to Clara's mother?" Marian asked, displaying a solicitude Jill had not expected. Marian too was badly shaken by the night's events.

"I'll see that she is taken care of," Frank replied, and did not go on to point out the thought that was in everyone's mind — if Clara's mother had not been so demanding herself, perhaps Clara's self-effacement would not have made her repress her true feelings toward others. But there were many "ifs" — and everyone was too upset and tired to do more than acknowledge the truth that after the fact "ifs" are futile.

One by one everyone except Jill and Don got up and left the kitchen. Each one absorbed in his own reaction to the terrible actions Clara's insane jealousy had provoked. Don reached over to take Jill's hand, to comfort and calm her.

"You won't leave now, will you? Are your feelings about this place all negative?" he asked.

"I am still stunned, but my feelings are hardly bad ones now that I know that it was poor mad Clara and not the whole town that hated me." A smile broke through the worried look and Jill impulsively leaned over to kiss Don. "Besides, I have a job here as Frank's assistant and will be able to star in your story-time productions at the pediatrics ward and —"

"Do you think you'll be too busy to do a little house hunting with me. I don't want to bring a bride to my bachelor quarters in town," Don said joyfully as he pulled her out of her chair and gave her a good hard squeeze and a long kiss.

Jill turned her head and replied in a throaty whisper, "Only if you think your bride will appreciate my impeccable taste —"

We hope you have enjoyed this Large Print book. Other G.K. Hall & Co. or Chivers Press Large Print books are available at your library or directly from the publishers.

For more information about current and up-coming titles, please call or write, without obligation, to:

G.K. Hall & Co.
295 Kennedy Memorial Drive
Waterville, ME 04901

Tel. (800) 223-1244
Tel. (800) 223-6121

OR

Chivers Press Limited
Windsor Bridge Road
Bath BA2 3AX
England
Tel. (0225) 335336

All our Large Print titles are designed for easy reading, and all our books are made to last.

0000106804271
LT FICTION ELL
Ellis, Julie,
Walk a tightrope /

HQ
MID-YORK LIBRARY SYSTEM
1600 Lincoln Avenue
Utica, New York 13502
(315) 735-8328

A cooperative library system serving
Oneida, Madison, and Herkimer Counties
through libraries and a bookmobile.

010100

A0000106804271